the 826 Quarterly

AN 826 VALENCIA ORIGINAL

Published May 2018
As the twenty-sixth volume of *the 826 Quarterly*.
Created by all hands on deck at 826 Valencia.

Mission Center

826 Valencia Street
San Francisco, California 94110

Tenderloin Center

180 Golden Gate Avenue
San Francisco, California 94102

826valencia.org

EDITOR Dana Belott
EDITORIAL BOARD Melissa Anguiano, Angelina Brand, Katie Cugno, Shelby Dale DeWeese, Kiley McLaughlin, Christina V. Perry, Kathleen Rodriguez, Ashley Smith, Ryan Young
DESIGN DIRECTOR Brad Amorosino
PUBLICATIONS MANAGER Meghan Ryan
BOOK DESIGNER Molly Schellenger
ILLUSTRATOR Cindy Derby
COPY EDITOR Christopher Keilman

PLEASE VISIT:
The Pirate Supply Store at our Mission Center
King Carl's Emporium at our Tenderloin Center
826valencia.org/store

ISBN 978-1-948644-02-0
Printed in Canada by Prolific Graphics
Distributed by Publishers Group West

the 826 Quarterly

VOLUME 26

*Published twice yearly, at least.

Contents

Bright as a Mango

True Humanity Means We're All Important

Hope Is a Blossom Tree

826 Valencia

Mystery!

SEJAL H. PATEL ✶ *Lawyer/Writer*

Do you know what I love most about my job? (I'm a lawyer, by the way.) It isn't that I get to say, "Objection!" That feels awesome, but that's not it. Guess again. It isn't that when I listen to people's stories, I shoulder some of their pain. Those parts of my job are amazing, but they aren't the best. Give up?

It's that every case is a *mystery*. Not just one big mystery, but thousands of mysteries, like a twenty-one-layer cake with different flavors in every layer. I never know what is going to happen. Who will I meet? What will they say? What did they do? What didn't they do? Will we win, lose, or come to some middle solution? When the case ends, what will happen to everyone as they scatter away into the wind? I love the mystery of it all because from start to finish, I hold on to a fuzzy purple blanket I call "hope"—hope that after all these grown-ups are done fighting, it's all going to be okay. That hope is the best thing about my job.

No one, and I mean *no one*, masters the art of mystery like the featured writers in this edition of *the 826 Quarterly*. I have been volunteering at 826 Valencia for years. I do it because after many years of doing my job, I suddenly felt tired one October day. I needed to take those smudgy lawyer glasses off and refill my imagination bucket. I thought, *who can refill my life with mystery so that I can help some upset grown-ups feel more hopeful? I need people who are clever, funny, wise, and inventive. Ah hah—kids!* That is my secret to being a great lawyer. Now you know.

As I was reading this work, I found myself wishing, hoping, and nail-biting (oh no, don't do that!) in mystery after mystery. We have, for example, mysteries about friendship. Asma A. writes in her poem that a star teases that black sky: "You are not as bright as me." The black sky responds, "You are making me feel sad and left behind." I know what this author is saying about differences, feeling "left behind," and courage. I wished, hoped, and bit my nails (NO!) that the black sky knew its power. Right here, mid-poem, was a mystery! The black sky laughs and says, "Without me, you wouldn't be as bright as you are now." "That is true. Black sky, without you, I wouldn't be bright," the star concedes. The star feels thankful for the black sky. And I put a daisy of hope in my inspiration bucket. Sophia K. writes about how close she is to her mother and how she has moved many times. She writes, "You have enough fresh starts and changes, and you have to figure out how to be okay with the parts of yourself you can't get rid of." Another daisy—here these authors are telling us that they know they are precious and never alone.

Then, there are the international mysteries. Keira V. squeezes into a giant, red envelope. What does she see? It is a mystery! She sees a big crowd with confetti all over and Chinese words and symbols. She is in China! Hilda H. writes that her grandmother came walking to San Francisco from El Salvador. That grandmother is my hero. How did she do that? These authors tell us about countries that are as much a part of them as America is. I know what they mean. My family is from India, but I was born in New York. I speak English, Spanish, and Gujarati. I feel like a stir-fry of so many ingredients. That's a mystery that we often think about, isn't it? *¡Claro que sí!* These writers taught me that these double and triple identities give our lives that much more richness. It's confusing in the most awesome kind of way. Add a few pink tulips to the bucket.

There also are the mystery-mysteries. Zach A. writes, "His hands clenched, flexed, and the shadows stuck tight to his skin like tar at his unique power's command." Oh boy, how are these characters going to work it out? Will the character in Amina F.'s piece be able to deliver the final line in the school play? She sure does! Laurence G. advises that if a black hole comes our way, we should do everything we would like to do "before it comes and devours us all." It's a good thing I am reading this amazing work now instead of saving it for later! Just when I am scared that these characters are doomed, the authors show me hope. Orange rose petals in the bucket.

With every flavor of mystery here—the chocolate bonanza layer, the lemon meringue layer, the kale banana with quinoa layer ("Ew, mom!" my kids would say, and I didn't even add the broccoli yet!)—these authors showed me the same hope I see in my law practice, the hope that everyone will be okay. We hear scary grown-ups fighting in the world, but thanks to young artists like these, I think everyone will be way more than just okay.

Sejal H. Patel *has been a public interest lawyer for about twenty years. Whoa. Yahir A. is right—that twenty years feels like only two! It took her a long time to find her way to writing. She started writing essays and fiction as a grown-up, after that inspiration bucket went empty. The editors of* Creative Nonfiction, The Rumpus, Literary Mama, *and* Harvard Divinity Bulletin *have been nice enough to publish her work. She has had plenty of rejection, too, but she keeps on writing. Like Opal the Bookworm, Sejal read millions and zillions of pages as a graduate of Northwestern Law School and Harvard Divinity School. School rocks! She lives in glorious San Francisco with her superhero daughters (uh oh, Lucia D.!) and her husband who just can't stop eating* La Luna de Queso *from Vanessa Perez's second grade class. Hey, man, save some for the rest of us! She also volunteers at 826 because she thinks what Kwan B. wrote is true about all 826 writers—on top of the world, you can never be beat!*

Stories invite us into someone else's experience: what's life like for a villain tired of dealing with superheroes who are "sooo annoying"? Or for someone who befriends a zombie and protects him from a hunter, saying, "Can you please not hunt my friend?" Or for a museum night guard and his friend? Here you will empathize with all kinds of characters and creatures and you may even find yourself changed when you emerge on the other side. ✳

Here the Seahorses Play Jazz

Fiction

(This Is Not) A Superhero Story

LUCIA D. * *age 10*
Buena Vista Horace Mann

Let's get this straight. I. Am. Not. A. Hero!

Eww.

Anyways, superheroes? They disgust me. Let's see, I prefer to be dressed all in black (no pink, eww!) and wearing boots up to my knees. No little heels, thank you very much!

I hate heroes! Why do they always defeat us? They make us look sooo bad! Like that one time Super Girl almost knocked me into tomorrow.

Ugh.

Yeah. So, my goal is to defeat a hero, which is not as easy as you think. I've tried so many times and never, ever have I defeated one.

But don't get me wrong. I'm a good villain.

Oh my gosh, superheroes are sooo annoying! They are all like, "Don't fear! Wonder Woman will save you," and all that blah, blah, blah. Such goody two shoes!

The next day...

Okay! I have a feeling today is the day. I "accidentally" hit Superman with my laser vision. He was all like, "You can't hurt me! I'm invincible!"

So I was all like, "Oh really?" Then I teleported behind him and pushed him with my super-strength. He was so confused about me disappearing that he didn't notice he was falling until he crash-landed on that grumpy lady's roof! Then I flew down and froze him into an icicle!

But then Wonder Woman, Super Girl, Black Widow, and Super Woman all came flying out of the sky to save their little "friend." I was all like, "Uh-oh," and was about to disappear when all the villains I knew appeared out of nowhere!

All the color drained from their faces and the superheroes looked like they were going to retreat. But before they could go, we beat them.

The next, next day . . .

Oh. My. Gosh. Did that really just happen? I think it did! We defeated the superheroes! I've made history!

To be continued . . .

Special Breathing Powers

MECHELL I. * *age 8*
Salvation Army Kroc Community Center

I have special breathing powers. It is cool because you can breathe underwater for days and years. I feel wet in my clothes. I see beautiful fish and jellyfish and sharks. The shark is as big as a tiger shark. I taste salty water and everything is as quiet as a stingray. I see curious divers and two shiny mermaids that talk to me. The mermaids have shiny tails and dresses. The mermaids say, "Hi, how are you doing?"

I see seahorses. They play jazz music and play trumpets and sea anemones. I see an anchor and I follow the anchor. It's as big as a big shark. It's rusty and heavy. It's attached to a boat. The boat is old, the boat is big, and the boat is as black as the night.

When I go back up to the surface, I tell my parents all about it! I say, "I saw curious divers, shiny mermaids, and seahorses. I saw sea anemones, sharks, and a rusty anchor that headed to a big, black boat."

Adventures of a Lonely Robot

MARCO C. * *age 9*
Buena Vista Horace Mann

There was once a lonely robot. He had one friend who was Geizel. They live in outer space together on a big rock. They go on an adventure to find hidden space treasure and find some. They use the treasure to buy an outer space mansion, jets, and food. They run out of money and they have to go find more treasure. They fly to Mars to find more.

They find a huge dragon protecting the treasure. They try to sneak in, but the dragon wakes up and they have to run away. They grab the treasure and leave quickly, but the dragon follows them. They lead the dragon into the sun, and the dragon and the sun explode.

The lonely robot and Geizel run away from the exploding sun. Geizel finds another robot named Kevin and all three become friends. They get more treasure, go home, and have a good night. The robot isn't lonely anymore.

Fame and Profit

ALLISON C. * *age 12*
Salvation Army Kroc Community Center

It was the year 2000 in Italy and Chef Boyardee and Alli were making a pot of their red, fancy, large, wide, noisy, bumpy, chunky, spicy, meaty, and tomato-y ravioli. "Mmm. Just the right amount of lamb and pepper."

"Oh, Chef. I think we shall sell our delicious, juicy, salty experiment," Alli said.

"If we do, we'll have to organize the money and who gets the brand name. Also, we have to get the FDA's approval, which takes a lot of work," said Chef Boyardee.

"I shall go to the FDA building and get their approval," Alli said.

"Okay, but first let us take a selfie to remember this!" shouted Chef Boyardee.

"Umm, what's a selfie?"

"Uhh, I actually don't know." The chef scratched his head. "Forget about that!"

As Alli went to get her keys, Chef Boyardee shouted, "WAIT!" Alli stopped in her tracks and turned around. "Who shall get the fame and profit?"

"Well first we have to get the FDA's approval or else there won't be any fame or profit."

Duhhh, Alli thought.

Alli drove down to the tall, white, large building. She entered the food to get tested. After two long, anxious weeks, the test results came back. It was approved.

"Now we shall discuss the fame and profit," Chef Boyardee said in a thick Italian accent. "I call fame!" Chef Boyardee shouted the same time as Alli said, "I call profit!" Both thought that was easier than anticipated.

After that, Chef got his face on a can of delicious food while Alli made thousands of dollars. Every now and then, Chef would get asked for a photo or autograph as Alli spent the money on ingredients for the canned food and buying whatever she wanted.

The end. (Note! This is *not* real!)

La Luna de Queso

MS. PEREZ'S SECOND GRADE CLASS
Cleveland Elementary School

Once upon a time there was a land called Melty Cheese Moon. On this moon there was a rocky cave that was super dark and big, but was locked away. Surrounding the cave were tall, yellow trees that were made of paper. The weather on Melty Cheese Moon was always snowy, and ice would fall from the sky every day. What many didn't know about this land was that there was a mysterious toilet that had hidden candy inside the toilet bowl.

One day, a fox named Troubles was getting ready to start her day. She brushed her blue and pink hair and put on her prettiest dress, which was made of water. As she finished getting ready, she thought to herself, *hmm, I miss being a human because I used to be able to eat all the yummy pizza in the world. Now I can only eat plants!*

Suddenly, Troubles had a thought! She thought about how the moon was made of cheese and pizza is also made of cheese so what if she just ate the moon? It probably tastes just like pizza. *Yum!* She excitedly did some backflips and cartwheels all around her home, *Barco de Queso,* which was actually a pumpkin house. Troubles got ready to start her plan of eating the delicious cheese moon.

However, on the other side of the Melty Cheese Moon lived the evil green and white monkey, I'Scream Banana

Man. The evil monkey spent his days climbing around his black wooden treehouse on top of a tall red and blue tree. Whenever he got bored, he would explore the moon and freeze people just by blinking his yellow and green eyes. After he would be done freezing people out of boredom, he would treat himself to some yummy Nutella and teleport back to his home. One day, I'Scream Banana Man thought to himself, *freezing people is starting to get kind of boring. It is time to do the most evil thing ever!*

The monkey then did an evil grin and came up with a plan to steal the hidden candy treasure! However, he had one problem. He realized that he would need a lot of energy if he wanted to steal that treasure. I'Scream Banana Man remembered that eating the cheese off of the moon would give him enough strength to fulfill his evil plan. So he set off to start eating the moon cheese.

Troubles had just gotten to the big rocky cave and was getting ready to eat the cheesy moon when she saw a furry monkey appear.

Troubles said to the evil monkey, "What are you doing here?"

I'Scream Banana Man responded, "I am here to eat all of the cheese off of this moon!"

Troubles gasped! They both wanted to eat the cheese but for different reasons. The monkey and the fox walked toward one another, each ready to devour the yummy cheese, when all of a sudden . . .

Zombie: The Attack!

HENRY A. ✳ *age 9*
Bessie Carmichael Elementary School

At the Chinese restaurant with my mom, I ate chow mein, chicken, and carrots. Then my mom said, "Carrots fight sickness."

Then zombies walked through the door because they smelled carrots and they wanted them for their brains so they could be alive again. "Give me carrots right now or I will haunt you."

I said, "Ah!" Then a zombie was going to attack a fat, chubby baby, so I jumped and pushed the baby out the way. Then I gave a carrot to a zombie and we became friends. The zombie became happy because he was alive again. The zombie looked like Michael Jordan and a small person. The zombie liked the carrot because it tasted like a warm chocolate marshmallow.

Then the zombie and I played basketball. I made a half-court shot on the zombie. Then I said, "Good game, Zombie."

While it was halftime, I ate a carrot. Then I went to see Zombie. He was gone, so I ate another carrot and used my super eyesight. I saw Zombie in the woods running from a hunter. The zombie said, "Can't catch me. You're slower than a turtle."

I went to the hunter and said to him, "Can you please stop hunting my friend? Even if he's a zombie, he's a good zombie. He didn't even attack me." I felt happy because the hunter stopped hunting him. I knocked his hands with a fist bump.

Learning from the Past

HAROLD M. ✳ *age 12*
Buena Vista Horace Mann

APRIL 14, 2017

Brriiinngg!

"Hurry up, or we will be late to history class," said Christian.

"Okay, class, today we are going to see a little movie about the march that took place in Washington, D.C. on August 28, 1963. Make sure to take notes because you will have a quiz about this tomorrow," said Ms. Morgan.

"Things haven't changed. I still see racism," said Christian.

"Well, it used to be worse back then. Martin Luther King Jr.'s life really changed people's minds," said Ms. Morgan.

Brriiinngg!

After class, Christian said, "Ms. Morgan, do you have a minute?"

"Sure, what's up?" said Ms. Morgan.

"The video that you showed us did not change the minds of Jamar, Mike, Aaron, or me," said Christian.

"Well, I guess you need to learn a little more," said Ms. Morgan. Then she took the TV out, but she did not use the same DVD. She got another one from her desk and slid it in the DVD player.

"I wonder if she's going to show us the same thing," said Jamar.

"Do you find this interesting, Ms. Morgan?" said Christian.

"Yes, I do," said Ms. Morgan.

"Say G.O.D.," said Jamar.

"G.O.D.," said Ms. Morgan.

Twenty minutes later, Ms. Morgan said, "Okay, I'm going to go to the bathroom. I'll be right back. Whatever you do, don't touch the glowing button on the DVD player."

Aaron was a very curious boy, so of course he pressed the button. At first it made a cracking sound, but then, *flooosh!*

A hole appeared in the TV, and in less than five seconds, they disappeared.

"Okay, I'm back," said Ms. Morgan.

"Guys?! I knew one of them was going to press it. Oh well, they will come back when they learn enough," said Ms. Morgan.

WASHINGTON, D.C., AUGUST 28, 1963

"What happened?" said Aaron.

"You touched something you were not supposed to," said Christian.

"Hey, what are you two $&%@ doing here?" said two white guys.

"You want to fight me? Catch me outside! How 'bout that?" said Christian.

"Christian, calm down, you don't need to fight," said Aaron.

"No, you don't understand. He called me a racist name because he was being mean and I'm going to rip his face off if he says something to me again," said Christian.

"Let's go," said Jamar.

They walked outside and heard people screaming, "No more racism against African Americans! We want equal rights!"

"Where are they going?" asked Mike.

"I don't know, but let's follow them," said Jamar. They followed the people through the streets to the Lincoln

Memorial. There were like 250,000 people waiting to listen to Martin Luther King Jr.'s speech.

"I have a dream!" said Martin Luther King Jr.

Twelve hours later . . .

"Did you guys learn enough?" asked Christian.

"Yeah," said Mike, Jamar, and Aaron.

Flooosh!

"Owww!" said Christian.

"Wow, you guys came back early! So, boys, did you learn enough?" asked Ms. Morgan.

"Yes, but did you tell us not to touch it just so we would touch it?" they all said with tired voices.

"Maybe, but tell me, what did you learn?" said Ms. Morgan.

"We learned that a lot has changed. It's not like it used to be back in the 1960s, and not everybody is racist," said Jamar.

"Well, it's good to know you learned something, and that you understand more," said Ms. Morgan.

My Cat's Adventure in the House

CAOILINN O. * *age 9*
Buena Vista Horace Mann

Hello, world! It is I, Saucey Cat! I am here to be lazy all day and wait on the blue bean bag until my owner comes back. All I dream about all day is food, outside, and play time, but also, naps on human-laps and naps on the blue bean bag.

I heard a noise coming from the kitchen! I ran to the kitchen to find a cucumber! "Ahhh! Run for your lives! It's a cucumber!" I pounced on it and I tried to eat it. It tasted like nothing, but it was still delicious.

I found some Tajín on the counter and I dumped it on the cucumber. I may have made a "small" mess. It tasted sour! I loved it! I finished the cucumber and was going back to the bean bag when I saw that the bathroom door was open. So I ran in and I started shredding toilet paper.

After two or three minutes, I heard the door open. It was my owners! I ran down the stairs to show them my master-piece of shredded toilet paper. Plus, it was in a mountain pile. Awesome! My owners ran up the stairs and saw my masterpiece. They saw it and started to clean it up. "No!" I meowed at them to tell them not to, but I don't think they understood me!

Later on, my owners and I ate dinner. I wanted more. I had mine earlier than theirs. Then my owners went to bed, so I did, too. I woke up in the middle of the night, and I walked into the kitchen. I saw an open bag of marshmallows falling onto the ground. I got confused by it. I thought they were called white mochi, and I ate all of the white marshmallows. They tasted good, but I didn't feel so good in the morning. The good thing was that I didn't spit up a hairball.

Today I learned that cucumbers are not predators and that I shouldn't eat a new bag of marshmallows straight. And that is what a day in the life of a cat is like when my owners are gone.

All about Buttermilk

KAYLIE G. * *age 10*
Epiphany Elementary School

Once, there was a girl named Buttermilk. She was in fifth grade and she was a normal size. She was at school and it was a great sunny day. At recess, students in her class made fun of her name, so then she got mad. In her thoughts, she felt like she wanted to tell on them, but she wanted to be brave and talk back. Then, she said to the students in her class, "What if someone made fun of your names and laughed at you? Would you like that?"

The students stopped talking and the students in her class were silent. They said, "No."

She said, "Alright then, don't be mean to other people's names or else they will be mean to you." The class was dismissed.

Buttermilk's parents picked her up at school and went to their home so that Buttermilk could finish her homework. Her dad was cooking dinner. When dinner was ready, Buttermilk's mom came home and they ate their dinner. Their dinner was spaghetti with meatballs. When dinner was finished, Buttermilk's parents told Buttermilk that they were superheroes and she gasped. She asked them if she was a superhero, too. So her parents said that she could be a superhero if she could control her emotions.

To be continued . . .

Morality in the Museum

ZACH A. ✳ *age 17*
The Marin School

At two in the morning on a Friday night, there were two individuals left in the museum and only one of them should've been there contractually. It was a pair of teenagers—young adults, really, one dressed in a simplistic security guard's uniform and the other in a mostly gray, semi-casual outfit. A 7-Eleven hotdog rested in the security guard's lap, and a thermos of brutally steaming tea in the other young person's hands. The pair sat in front a complex, abstract piece of art that went from ceiling to floor with only an inch or two above and below to spare.

The security guard took a bite of his hotdog, spilling ketchup onto his name tag—*Jason*. The man's last name was half-covered by tangy sauce. He let out an annoyed little huff and swiped it off of the metal with an irritated glimmer in his dark eyes.

"Should we not be, like, eating? This late at night, at least?" Jason asked, swallowing down an only half-chewed bite of food and wincing just for a moment. "I know eating past eight or whatever is bad, but I only actually feel bad about eating *this* late at night—or, this early in the morning. I dunno, Zero."

Since it's way past eight, Zero signed at Jason, *I'm just going to assume it's bad. Plus, you're on duty.* A hesitation in the movement of their hands and Zero sighed almost inaudibly. *Honestly, you should be more concerned about someone coming in and firing you for hosting me on your watch like this is a totally legal teen hangout.*

"I'll just tell this theoretical manager or whoever that you're interested in being a guard as well. And, of course, if it's someone breaking in, it's better to have two folks instead of just the one."

You think your manager is going to believe a five-foot-one mute kid like me wants to be a security guard? Zero raised an eyebrow as Jason stuck out his tongue instead of responding. *I mean, if they're that gullible . . .* Zero's hands paused in their conversation to snag a fun-sized Twix from the shared bag of Halloween candy.

"They probably are," Jason agreed, taking another bite of his hotdog and chewing it thoroughly before he swallowed and spoke again, "plus, let's be real, my dude. My manager is sound asleep! She's not comin' to snoop in on what I'm doing when I'm protecting the art. If anyone comes butting in, it'll be a villain, and we'll kick their butt. Or, butts, maybe. Who knows."

It'll just be you kicking butt, I hope you know.

"What?" Jason glanced to Zero, a mock-offended expression on his freckled face as he pressed one gloved hand to his chest and gasped. "You mean, you're not going to kick butt with me?"

My power doesn't kick butt like yours does. It's defensive. How many times have we gone over this?

"You could make it offensive," the hand cupped dramatically over Jason's heart dropped down, grasping for an energy drink and raising it to take a lazy sip, "and you know that! Just say the word—literally—and drop some poor criminal into the middle of nowhere. You could literally put any supervillain you can touch into space."

I'm not going to.

"Boo-hoo. Your hero alias should be 'No-Fun'." That was complete with arrogant air quotes.

How about: 'Captain No-Murder-On-My-Teenage-Consciousness? Or maybe, 'Commander Lots-Of-Warrants-For-My-Arrest'?

Jason just squinted in annoyance, staring at Zero's square pupils as his pierced lips tugged open for a no-doubt amazing retaliation—but that was cut off at the sound of something heavy thumping on the floor, echoing enough for someone to instantly know it was in another room. Both young individuals stopped their playful bickering to immediately look toward the open archway to their left, intent on peering through the darkness and seeing what had made any sort of noise. A fruitless endeavor, sure, but they both found it necessary. Just in case they actually could see something.

Zero's hands raised, drawing Jason's now sharpened attention.

What was that.

"Don't draw on clichés, Zero," Jason muttered to his companion, the shadows of the room they resided in beginning to squirm across the floor and cling to the amateur security guard's arms as Jason slowly maneuvered onto his feet as quietly as he could. His hands clenched, flexed, and the shadows stuck tight to his skin like tar at his unique power's command. Zero stood as well, taking the time to stuff a handful of candy into one of their thousands of pockets. Jason made a face at Zero before looking towards the leftmost room, letting the shadows glue to his upper body and darken the already black outfit. No light reflected from him.

Are you gonna reprimand me for clichés, and then go into a pitch-black room to see what could've made that noise? Really, Jason? Zero signed in annoyance.

"The difference is that this is my job. Seeing what's up in that room over there is what I get paid to do. You're just jinxing us," Jason near-silently replied, creeping toward the archway as his companion scoffed inaudibly and followed close behind. Zero's albino hand hovered by their headstrong friend's back, ready to grab Jason and disappear with a word if they deemed the situation necessary of immediate evacuation. As smart as Jason was, the man considered no situation too much for him, so Zero had to play his fight-or-flight reaction.

The pair approached at a perfectly slow and quiet pace, oozing over the floor like a snail on a straight path through the archway before Jason suddenly jerked to the side and hid just beyond the edge of the archway. Zero stood in the center of the door frame's outline, startled and stuck like a deer in the headlights, before they dove to the side as well and glared with white irises at Jason. He was on his phone.

Oh my god, what are you doing.

No response.

Jason.

Nothing, again, as Jason's thumbs quickly tapped over the screen of his phone. Zero smacked their friend's head and snapped Jason's attention from the device to his scowling companion and their speedy hands.

Jason, what the hell.

"Dad sent a text—asked if I fed my share of the dogs. You know he'll be a pain if I don't respond, and we don't want him callin' us in the middle of a fight, right? I don't, at least." At the sound of a hand meeting flesh, Jason looked up, staring at where Zero had pressed their palm to their face in endless annoyance. "What?"

I'm pretty sure your life isn't real, Jason.

"Shut up, I'm almost done." A few seconds later and Jason stuffed his phone back into his pocket, zipping it up securely and then checking his shadow-slathered knuckles in preparation. "Okay. Dad's satiated, for now, and now we can go in and find out what's up. You ready?"

I mean, no.

"Perfect."

The Mark

RUBY E. ✳ *age 11*
Buena Vista Horace Mann

I yank my sister down the street, dodging children playing hopscotch and crisply dressed businesspeople as we hurry home. "Slow down," my sister Lynn says, panting. "I need to check Snapchat."

She pulls her hand out of my grasp, smooths down her long brown hair, and starts snapping selfies, pausing every few seconds to change filters.

"You have *got* to be kidding me," I say. "You know Mom will kill us if we get home late." I am not overreacting when I say my mom will kill us. She is basically a rabid cheetah in ten-inch heels.

Finally, I get my sister home. My mother greets us at the door, slumped against the wall, her eyeballs rolling around in her head.

"Lynnnnnnnn, Artemiaaaaaaaaaa," she says. Her voice is thick, and whether it is with excitement or hate, I can't tell. "Tonight you must go." I know what she means. Tonight we will have to go to the cemetery.

As Lynn and I walk down the street, a feeling of dread settles over me. The same street that was so alive two hours ago is now deserted, the full moon casting shadows over the whole block. Lynn is talking on her phone (loudly) about makeup and fashion, and why she hates Valentino (because of his new line of hats made entirely of feathers). I quicken my pace, my feet shooting along the sidewalk. Then we reach the graveyard.

The graveyard gate is made of metal, probably iron, maybe steel, with ravens and crows etched into the handle. "I hate this place," Lynn says. She is carrying a large basket of flowers. We arrive at the first grave and we toss the flowers on the graves. Suddenly, I hear a noise behind me. I spin around, momentarily blinded by my own hair. My heart is thumping loudly, and adrenaline courses through me. I hear a scream, and Lynn crashes to the ground next to me. Something hits my face. Then everything goes black.

When I come to, something blue and shimmery floats over me. It turns out to be a short, mad-looking lady. Her face is shimmery blue with long, stringy brown hair. She extends her (blue) arm to reveal long red nails that are dripping. She whispers in my ear, "You smell like a dead person." She wrinkles her nose, making her look like a blue ferret. She smirks at me. "You were really easy to take down. One hit, and you were out." She laughs, and it sounds like an elephant fighting a very mad T-rex.

"Where's Lynn?" I croak, blood spilling from the wound in my leg.

"The other girl? Oh, we don't want her. She is of no use to us. You, however, are a different story. You have The Mark." Then she erupts into a cloud of flames.

I see a new lady standing in front of me, this one much creepier. She looks like a zombie mixed with that one queen lady who liked cake. She says, "You have The Mark." She points at my arm, to a small round circle. She giggles. "I cannot let you go." Then she touches my arm, and my head explodes.

No one ever sees me again.

She hated cake.

Opal the Bookworm vs. the Monster of Illiteracy

OPAL JANE R. ✶ *age 14*
Ruth Asawa School of the Arts

Da-da-da-DA(fanfare)!

The superhero Opal Jane the Bookworm has come to save the world from the dank, evil-smelling prison of illiteracy, and all other enemies of literature who shun the glorifying presence of books.

(Old fashioned ring tone here.)

Oh look, the Bookworm-in-Need phone is ringing! An innocent academic is in danger!

Opal the Bookworm rushes to the phone. "Hello, this is Grannie McGee. My son is in terrible danger! He went down into the basement to watch TV, and has not come back up since! Once I tried to take him back upstairs, and he destroyed half the books in my library. Boo-hoo-hoo."

"Don't worry," Opal Jane responds, "this looks like a job for Opal the Bookworm!"

Da-da-da-da-da-da-da-da-Da-DA! Opal the Bookworm rockets into the front lawn of a well-cared-for building, and an older lady rushes out.

"Oh, thank you, Opal the Bookworm!" she exclaims with relief. "My grandson is in the basement!"

Opal the Bookworm rushes inside, not expecting what is lying in wait for her in the depths of the deep, dark basement. *Da-da-da-DA (foreboding music).* Bravely she descends the basement stairs, not knowing that she is entering the lair of her worst enemy!

Opal the Bookworm pauses at the bottom of the stairs. She smells the odiferous smell of imbecility and ignorance. In other words, it smells like a mountain of stinky socks. The brave Bookworm advances, fearing nothing.

Oh, no! Opal the Bookworm spots something deeper in the basement. It is a page torn from a book!

Opal the Bookworm feels deeply torn, exactly like the page must feel when it was brutally torn from its correct place in its book. She feels deep sympathy for the discarded page. She was once discarded like a page ripped from a book.

"This is a crime against all humanity," Opal the Bookworm solemnly declares as she holds the torn page in her hand. "I have sworn to fix this, and end the scourge of literary unawareness across the world. And I will!"

She tucks the mangled page safely into her pocket, which is bigger on the inside than it is on the outside. It can fit an infinite amount of stuff, which is handy for a superhero to have.

Then she notices another battered page laying on the ground, then another, then another, then another. So the papers go on, making a trail to what surely must be the location of the monster. She eagerly follows them, ready to defeat the deserving monster.

She finally reaches the end of the trail, and notices the flickering glow of a TV screen. Aha! There is the monster! A large lump is outlined by the lights of the flat screen TV. Lazing in front of the television, possessing innocent children, and destroying books left and right.

Fortunately, Opal the Bookworm has come prepared.

From her magical pocket she removes the Newspaper of Doom. This is no ordinary newspaper. It delivers bad news to enemies of the written word everywhere.

To be used properly, the Newspaper of Doom has to be thrown atop the person/thing it is tasked to vanquish. Upon contact with the enemy, it shrinks the person/thing into a size that it can easily fold up into itself.

Needless to say, once you're in the Newspaper of Doom, it is very hard to get out.

While activating the Newspaper of Doom, Opal the Bookworm examines the monster closely.

It is a terribly ugly monster. It is vaguely slug-shaped, and a sickeningly glistening deep brown color. On each side it has approximately ten arms and legs that are completely disproportionate to its body.

Inside the semi-transparent, slimy body can be seen floating the body of what must be Granny McGee's grandson. It appears that said Monster of Illiteracy has swallowed the hapless grandson.

Opal the Bookworm narrows her eyes at the faint shape, and she is determined to save him from what must be an unilluminated and sticky existence inside the monster.

Suddenly, the slug-like monster rises up from its seat in front of the television! It finally has noticed Opal the Bookworm!

"Roaaaaaaaar," it roars quite impressively while dramatically waving its upper body around. "Opal the Bookworm, we meet again. Last time we met, you stopped me from possessing some blameless adults to have a mass burning of Harry Potter books. This time I will defeat you!"

It pulls one of its many hammy arms back to strike Opal the Bookworm. Unfortunately for the monster, Opal the Bookworm is a strong believer in nonviolence. She knows the Newspaper of Doom is a peaceful way to be rid of your enemies without having to harm them at all.

So she throws the newspaper on top of the monster.

Now, it is slightly disconcerting to see an oversized slug thing with about ten arms on each side be swallowed by a newspaper, but it can be done. That is exactly what happened to the monster when Opal the Bookworm vanquished it.

While the Newspaper of Doom neatly disposed of the Monster of Illiteracy, there was a great suctioning noise, and a slightly slimy person-shaped thing emerged.

There sat a thankful and exalted looking teenager who said, "Thank you for saving me from that evil monster who possessed me, Opal the Bookworm!"

Here the story ends, with the Monster of Illiteracy vanquished for the present.

But there is a new dot on the horizon of good literature: E-book Girl: sidekick or enemy?!

Hannah Saves the Day!

JACQUELINE G. * *age 12*
Buena Vista Horace Mann

On Marin Street in Rosemont, Pennsylvania, there was a big white house with a pool. This was where Hannah lived. She didn't have family members in Pennsylvania. She lived there because her college had given her a career placement to be a doctor. Hannah also worked there in college.

She came home from her job as a doctor and turned on the TV. She put on ABC and went to the kitchen. Then the reporter said, "On Friday, there's going to be a bombing in Birmingham, in the Birmingham Church. You should come on Friday to stop the bombing."

Hannah dropped the glass of water she was holding and it crashed on the floor. She felt panicked and she said to herself, "I should save the world."

Hannah took a bath and packed her clothes. She got her map and locked her house. Then Hannah drove to Birmingham. It took four days to get to Birmingham. Hannah came on Friday at 7:30 a.m. The bomb was going to explode later that day, at 6:00 p.m. Hannah had time to save the Birmingham Church.

Hannah went to Woolworth's to buy supplies to protect herself. When Hannah entered, she saw on the TV that people were protesting. People were getting hurt because the police were hitting at them. Hannah felt stressed and started to get supplies to protect herself.

Later, she got into her car and just drove. She went to a restaurant and got a drink. She saw the news on TV and noticed that it was 5:00 p.m. She drank her sweet orange juice and ran to the car. She drove and she stopped at a bathroom and got her suitcase to protect herself. She looked at her Apple Watch and it was 5:30 p.m. Hannah had thirty minutes to protect herself.

Hannah went to the church in Birmingham. Hannah wanted to get everything under control. It was 6:00 p.m.

Hannah ran and saw a man with bomb. She pushed him. She only had thirty seconds to stop the bomb. The man was on the floor. She got the bomb and used her billy club to break the bomb. Hannah hit the bomb like a baseball. The bomb sounded like an airplane as it flew away.

People were outside the church and watched how she stopped the bomb. She saw everybody cheering her on. The reporters put Hannah on the news. The headline said, "The Woman Who Saved the Day in Birmingham."

The Legend of the Stolen-Bite Peach

FAVIO N. * *age 12*
James Lick Middle School

Long, long ago, an emperor called Zu was the Son of the Heavens because he was somehow related to the Immortal Queen Mother of the Heavens. But the Queen still looked down upon Zu. For the Emperor's sixteenth birthday, the Queen went to visit him. Unicorns burst from a cloud with the Queen. The light of the stars on the Queen's crown was brighter than every lantern. The peach was the one thing that everyone looked at when she arrived.

"Zu," the Queen said. "For your birthday, I will grant you the wish of immortality. So I bring the peach of longevity. This peach will grant you 999 more years of life."

The Queen had a servant to take the peach to the emperor. Then the unicorns leapt into the sky. For a moment, everyone at the party only stared at the heavens. The emperor, already licking his lips, commanded his peach to be brought to him. The crowd was all looking at the servant in silence. The sweet smell of the peach wafted through the air as if it were intoxicating wine. Right when the peach was in the emperor's reach, someone snatched the peach out of the servant's hand! The stunned moment was silent, then the emperor told his guards to retrieve his peach at once. When they tackled the man to the floor, the emperor was stunned. When the peach rolled over to him, it was bitten. It was a surprise who was the thief. It was the magistrate who was distantly connected to the emperor by marriage.

He roared, "How dare you take a bite of my peach! I should have you killed at once!"

"But how can I be killed if I already took a bite of the peach?" the thief said.

"Fool, it only gives you lives. It doesn't make you invincible," said the emperor.

"But what would the Queen of Heavens think, that she gave you time to become worthy of immortality? What would she think if you just sent me to death?" the thief said.

After a silent pause, the emperor finally said, "Grr . . . just take him away."

The guards took the thief away. The emperor was thinking how much the better the peach would have tasted if it wasn't bitten.

Inspired by The Legend of the Stolen-Bite Peach.

A Giant, Red Envelope

KEIRA V. ✳ *age 11*
Boys and Girls Club — Tenderloin Clubhouse

On Lunar New Year, I was on my tablet playing *Buddyman* on my bed. Right in the middle of my game, the doorbell rang and startled me only a bit. I ran to open the door, but nobody in the house could answer the door. In fact, my mom was taking a nice, warm shower. And I could hear water splatter once I passed by her room.

The first thing I saw was the mailman. "A package for Keira V.," he said. And right before my eyes, he pulled out a giant, red envelope! When I asked him where it was from, he said it was a secret until I opened it. And he told me to step aside and hold the door open.

All I saw was one really red rectangle slip. I gasped, and then I said, "Goodbye," and, "Thank you." And then I quickly pushed the large shape all the way to my room to reveal the surprise.

I shut the door and grabbed my mother's envelope opener. I took a few minutes opening about seventeen or twenty inches of the side. It finally revealed a bright light, and a tiny note stuck out of it.

I pulled it out and read it. It said that it was from a magical wizard in Alcatraz who knows me, but I don't know him.

And apparently he was my special ancestor. He told me a little bit about his hat, and what he wears for a wizard. He told me to go into the envelope for a special surprise.

I squeezed into the envelope, and the first thing I saw was a big crowd with lots of confetti all over. And then I saw lots of buildings with Chinese symbols and words. *Am I in China?* I thought.

I went forward into the crowd, and I saw a giant dragon! It looked about six feet long! There were millions of dancers everywhere! There were fireworks, too.

It was a Chinese New Year!

Part One: The Call to Darkness

KHALIL L. ✳ *age 15*
Homeschool

"Heed my warning and I may grant thee a single cherry from the tree outside," she said. The boy glanced beyond the kitchen window, beholding an old and weathered cherry tree. Its trunk was tall and slender, with bright green leaves and vines that had infused themselves into its branches years ago. Now they'd even come to wind themselves around its dark brown frame. From each branch, hung a single bright red cherry that only grew more luminescent in the rays of the evening sun.

"But mother, this tree is plain and of haggard appearances. Can you not see how it withers?" the boy shouted, pointing an accusing finger towards a subdivision of cold and gray branches as they were grimly strangled by their accompanying vines.

"It surely provides not what I seek. Please, I must know the nature of *this* vessel!" he begged, reaching for the box still on top of the kitchen counter. But he was unable to lay even a finger on it as his mother held him back. Seeing that her child's suborn nature would not allow him to yield, she opted to constrict his persistence the best way she knew how—with magic.

The little boy's mother used her wand to lift the box thirty feet into the air with the sole intention of sending it to the tallest cupboard in all of the mansion. The box lingered in the air for a second or two, just one centimeter below the ceiling before she slowly guided it into the cupboard where its door slammed shut. But the boy was a far cleverer and cunning child than he'd led his mother to believe. Not even magic would keep him from knowing the secrets of the box.

In the middle of the night, while the house was still and his mother had already drifted off into her world visions, the boy snatched her wand from her bed stand. He then made his way back to the kitchen and proceeded to begin his work. Unsure of his ability to keep the box suspended in midair long enough for him to grasp it, the boy decided to forge a chaotic hill of sloppily stowed clothing and clumsily placed furniture all stacked against the kitchen walls leading to the cupboard.

With her wand, he called an arsenal of brown dining chairs. Old and burrowed into by age, the sheer force of the wand might send them smashing into the kitchen walls, the result of which left a carnage only recognizable as the debris of a battlefield. He called the piano to add to the cataclysm, a deafening crash erupting from the collision. The golden tendrils from within the shallow depths of the piano's body sprang out, wrapping around several severed chair legs that'd logged themselves into the wall, in a crude attempt to construct a sustainable hold on the emerging calamity.

The boy continued to add couches from the living room and family room that crushed each other, then boxes and crates from storage rooms that were smashed against those couches upon impact. Even the kitchen's own plates, cups and bowls could not escape the wand's call, as several shards of strayed wood and glass fusing with each other as they came raining back down to the surface.

With subtle haste, he began to climb the textured wooden hilltop, loose books and pillows clattering and plopping on the floor as he used them as stepping stones. As he continued to climb, he grabbed a weathered old boot that hadn't been so strongly planted within the pile. Without the strength of the heap to hold it in place, the boot was pulled from the hill. With no hands to call any other surface home, his right hand still clutching the boot and his left sustaining a three-fingered grip on his mother's wand, the boy fell from the halfway-climbed mountain of clutter, sprawling in midair. The wand flew from his grasp, the air sending it twirling out of his view.

He screamed out in terror, his body rapidly cutting through the long distance between cupboard and the cold stone floor. But before his body could collide with the ground, from far beyond, he heard the sound of his mother's voice chanting an incantation new to his ear.

"Prohibere Procidens!" she cried. When he landed, the boy was surprised to find that his body had come to rest safely upon a bed of air. Immediately, the boy recognized the true nature of his lost grip on the wand. His mother had guided it from his grasp and into her own. As his mother slowly lowered the boy back down to the floor, hollow cries began to echo out into the halls. They both glanced outside the window, only to see the tree's cherries glowing with a bright red flame as if it were screaming out in fear of what was to come next.

While the boy had never come close enough to lay claim to the box, his fall had sent a shockwave through the mass. Subsequently, the shockwave had loosened the box just enough to rattle it free from the cupboard and send it toppling down the hillside of furnishings and other household appliances. The boy scurried to where it lay, locked under a hard wooden chair and an ornate light blue rocking cradle.

"No!" his mother cried out, but by the time the word had even reached his ears, it was already too late. The boy looked inside, puzzled to behold a small golden crystal coated in small blotches of red. His attention was ripped back to his mother as she collapsed to her knees.

Her hand had even already relinquished her wand, both clasped around her temple. Suddenly, one of the inky red spots began to sink into the crystal's golden surface and a theory was forming in the boy's mind. He darted to his mother, crystal still in hand. When he reached her, the boy's heart was consumed in terror, his growing hypothesis being granted recognition as he gazed into her eyes. In one last moment of letting clarity, she called her wand to her hand. But even the boy could sense it was too late.

Each dot that sank into the crystal saw another drop of crimson growing in her own hazel eyes. Every drop that appeared in her eyes saw each spell she cried out in hope of alleviating the crystal's power being twisted into a coarse profanity. But then, a new throng of words began to pour out from her lips.

"Worthless stupid child! For all your potential, you've understood nothing. All the power you might've once gained at my side, wasted!" The boy was awe-stricken. His own mother, her eyes consumed in blood, now spoke words to him he'd once thought unimaginable of her. He knew it was the crystal. He knew it had somehow latched itself to her mind, wrenched out every piece of her true existence. It seemed to be the most logical conclusion for her switch in character. But then, perhaps every insult she continued to spit at him was true. The thought couldn't help but take to the center of his mind. From the destruction of his mother's soul to the very day he was born, he'd caused nothing but pain to her. He'd been nothing but a selfish burden to her, and now she would pay the price for it.

"Look at what you've done to me! I tried to protect you, to spare you from the darkness and now . . ." The boy could feel his heart crumbling under the weight of her words. The last spot submerged itself into the crystal. He dropped his head to her knee, the crystal still in his lap, one spot remaining.

The First Superhero

JOSHUA A. ✳ *age 9*
Bessie Carmichael Elementary School

"Oh no! There is a hurricane!" said my mom. My mom gave me hot soup with beans. I tried it and it was really good. I took another scoop. When I finished eating, I ran to my bed.

"Ahhh!" I screamed, and I went to my mom because I was very scared. I went to my mom, shivering and trying to run as fast as I could. Then when I got to her, I started noticing that I got really fast.

My mom looked at me and was amazed that I got super speed. My mom was very shocked. She was so shocked that she wanted me to try to stop the hurricane. My grandma was scared that I would burn, so she made me a special fireproof suit so I wouldn't burn.

The hurricane got stronger. There were people driving near the hurricane. Then I ran to the hurricane, running the opposite way it was spinning. I stopped the hurricane and everyone was very happy. Everyone was cheering because I stopped the hurricane.

Then the sky got clear. Then everyone could see the stars and the moon. After that night I started selling the soup with beans. I started selling suits like mine. I helped people again and again. I helped people anywhere in the world.

Eat Bok Choy and Save the Day

MAYA M. * *age 9*
Bessie Carmichael Elementary School

"I am scared!" I said to my mom. My mom was busy making *sinigang*, my favorite dish. When she was done making it, I pulled out a spoon. Then I pulled out a fork from the container full of spreaders, forks, knives, and spoons. The utensils rattled while I pulled out my spoon and fork. After I pulled them out, I started eating it.

Suddenly, I heard lots of thunder and lightning! I ate my sinigang super fast. I ate as much sinigang as I could, then I flopped back down in our black comfy couch. Suddenly, I heard more thunder! I jumped up and looked out the window. I almost forgot that the hurricane was coming. I quickly ran to the kitchen and peeked into the refrigerator to see if there was yogurt. I saw *kari kari!* I totally forgot we had the kari kari! I took the bowl of the kari kari and ate the bok choy. I left the meat and rice out.

When I ate the bok choy, I immediately grew taller, then a little fatter. The bok choy had a white stem and lots of leaves that were as green as grass. When I grew big, I felt a little bit stronger. My left foot went to Texas and my right foot went to Florida.

But I forgot there was lightning and thunder. It was so close to shocking me, but I dodged it! I was very lucky! I was also a little bit worried that I would step on some buildings. Immediately, the hurricane stopped! So, whenever a hurricane hits, I will eat bok choy and save the day!

¿Quién dijo que yo no sabía? "Who said I didn't know?" these young authors ask. And in their writing, they reveal their rebuttal: *we know a lot, and we're willing to share it*. Diving into memories, personal experiences, and musings, these narratives preserve family histories, challenge stereotypes, and capture triumphant game-winning free throws. Be ready to listen and learn. ✳

¿Quién Dijo que Yo No Sabía?

Personal Narratives

Unorthodox Riches

SOPHIA K. * *age 15*
John O'Connell High School

You know how people go on midnight taco runs, or visit the local 7-Eleven for peanut M&Ms and a rainbow Slurpee in the middle of the night? When you're still awake because you just are, and you're having an intense food craving for something just downright unusual? You know what I'm talking about? Well, my version of that was glazed doughnuts at midnight. It was a well-known fact in the town that I lived in at the time that there was a place that had amazing doughnuts at any time of the day. The little shop in the middle of a mechanic's parking lot was always open at midnight, making them fresh, hot, and deliciously diabetic. It was around that time that I had started to inherit my mother's nocturnal instincts. No matter how hard I tried to fall asleep, how early I had been up the morning before, I was always awake until the early hours of the morning, restless and jittery, with an impossible craving for adventure. So, my mother and I would get into our old beat-up minivan that had been through more than a war veteran, sporting pajamas that were embarrassing to say the least, and take a drive. We would drive around, challenging each other to figure out how to get to a certain destination without using the freeway, blasting the radio on the oldies station. We would drive through the really rich suburban areas and laugh at how pretentious they always looked. We always ended up at the doughnut shop, though. On those nights, it was like we owned the world. We could forget whatever it was that was troubling us and just breathe. The memories of those good times were what got me through the bad ones. They were and are one of the reasons that me and my mother are so close. Those times are something that not many people get a chance to have, and I am incredibly grateful for them.

When I was younger I moved a lot, too many times to count. I was in and out of regular and homeschool for varying reasons. By the time I was fourteen, I had been to eight different schools. While it sounds kind of lonely and a bit tumultuous, it helped me to cultivate the dexterity to be comfortable in my own skin and with being on my own. You have enough fresh starts and changes, and you have to figure out how to be okay with the parts of yourself you can't get rid of. Starting at a new school, being the new kid had become a really familiar and almost comfortable situation. The first couple of days would always be the same. Trying to learn everybody's names (making a few people angry with my mistakes along the way), understanding the routine that specific school had, and just getting my bearings of my new surroundings. When you've done it as many times as I've had to, you learn how to catch on quickly, a skill which you can apply to pretty much anything. By the time those first few days were up, though, I would always have a couple of people who I could call friends—another skill that comes with practice. Those experiences that were born out of necessity have given me a sense of navigation and a comfort of being in uncomfortable situations, that I know can only serve me well in the rest of my life.

Misunderstood Young Man from the Streets

RUBEN E. * *age 16*
John O'Connell High School

Being a young black man growing up in San Francisco, life isn't always so easy. But, that's my power. I hold experiences and perspectives that others can't and I see things a lot of people don't see every day. I believe I will be successful, not in spite of, but because of my identity. In terms of cultural wealth, I have acquired aspirational, social, and navigational capital through my life, due to my sister's success, my participation in the Black Student Union (BSU), and my experiences living in the 'hood.

At my school, we have programs such as BSU which is run by Ms. Mya. Mya is one of the most helpful people when it comes to school. She helped my sister get to where she is and I plan on using her help to get me there as well. I learned so much about my roots and my ancestors from BSU. I also appreciate BSU because they showed me something I thought I'd never seen, which was a school I felt accepted in. Last year, Mya took me on a Historically Black College and University (HBCU) tour and I enjoyed it. During the HBCU tour, I toured several colleges, toured the cities, and had fun with my friends in North and South Carolina. I was exposed to black college life, which excited me and pushes me to go to school every day.

The world views me as just another statistic, as if I'm going to be gone tomorrow. When I say the world, I am talking about anyone that hasn't been through the same struggles that I have. Because of this, I feel like I have to work twice as hard to be successful. When I'm around, I can feel when some people aren't comfortable by my presence. Me being a strong young black man, I do not let it bother me. I plan to be successful in the future, which looks like me doing something I love for the rest of my life, without falling into society's traps.

The One-Way Ticket to Embarrassment

AMINA F. * *age 14*
Gateway Middle School

Your school play is almost at its end. Now it is time for your line, the one that the play director assigned to you and to which you reluctantly agreed.

You clear your throat, getting ready to recite your piece. You try, but all you can manage to choke out is "... uuuh."

Feel the tension. Everyone is staring at you.

"They're judging me," the scant voice whispers in your ear. You shush it, eager to stop it before it becomes rampant.

You think to yourself, *Remember the words of your best friend: "Imagine the audience all uniformly dressed in neon yellow shower caps and toddler swimming goggles, singing 'Head, Shoulders, Knees, and Toes,' while juggling rubber chickens."* You try to hold yourself back and brush the picture out of your head, but you can't. You do the worst thing that anyone like you on the stage can do.

You giggle.

Ugh. How foolish! You have forbidden yourself from giggling many times, and you know why? Your giggle sounds like a hyena attempting to sing in a soprano voice, that's why. Then the thought occurs to you: *I just giggled.*

No.

Your face turns the shade of a cranberry.

You smile to yourself when the solution hits you. Remember those Scaredy the Squirrel books that your teacher would read to your class every single day? Follow Scaredy's advice: when in doubt, play dead.

But you don't.

You say your well-rehearsed line. "And they all lived happily ever after."

Well, not so much.

My Family Tree

KEILY P. * *age 12*
Herbert Hoover Middle School

Years ago, my mom and my dad met in Peru. Later, my parents found love. They found love in Lima, Peru when they were in their early twenties. They moved to San Francisco when they were twenty-one years old. In 1998, my older brother was born. In 2005, I was born, and in 2009, my younger brother was born. My older brother's name is Marco. My younger brother's name is Christian, and my dad's name is Marco.

My mom wants me to go to get my suitcases. My mom said, "Keily, let's go. We're going to be late." Keily is my name and my mom's name is Bertha. What my mom is trying to say is that I have to hurry so my family and I won't miss our flight. The reason I'm leaving San Francisco, California is because my family and I are going to Peru.

The reason I'm going to Peru is because every summer I go to visit my family members and my ancestors to see how they are doing in life. My favorite thing about going to Peru is getting to hang out with my family and to travel to other cities in Peru. My family and I stayed in Peru for a month and celebrated Christmas and New Year's Eve.

My Place from Before

PEDRO D. * *age 11*
Everett Middle School

I know that we are from Mexico. I like Mexico because we lived next to a store with good food and got to live good and go to the shop. They would sell anything to us. We got to go anywhere in Mexico. We ate pizza with ketchup with our family and played games. Uncles bought me anything.

Family, Name, and Language

MARCELA R. * *age 15*
John O'Connell High School

When I think of Christmas, birthdays, or parties, I think of presents and joy, but I also remember foods like my mother's delicious *tamales de puerco*, which is a Salvadoran dish made of pork and *masa*. I remember at a young age, maybe seven, my mother would tell me to sit down and cut *los hilos para los tamales*. As an innocent little seven-year-old, being told to cut the strings felt like a huge responsibility. *Tamales* and *pupusas con curtido*, which was kind of like a stuffed pancake with cabbage on the side, were the main foods served at our huge Salvadoran get-togethers, no matter if it was Christmas or if we were just celebrating a cousin's birthday. When I think of cultural wealth I think of my family, especially my mother, because not only do they all love me dearly, but they help me grow in many cultural aspects.

When I think of linguistic wealth, I think of my name, not Marcela, but Sochilt. If you were to search for my name it would immediately autocorrect to Xochitl, because it is spelled wrong, but on purpose. My mother would tell me to not pay attention to the way people pronounced it or spelled it. It's pronounced (soh-chee-t), but many people have their own way of saying it. When I was younger, I used to hate the fact that everyone had a nice name that everyone could pronounce. Attendance was my worst fear because every teacher would say it wrong and then it would be a room full of loud obnoxious kids laughing at the mispronunciation of Sochilt. Once I sat down with my mother and asked her, "I don't understand why you named me 'Sochilt' if no one can say it or spell it, and even you don't know the meaning." She looked at me and laughed, which irritated me because she did not understand my annoyance. She responded with, *"¿Quién dijo que yo no sabía qué significaba? Y yo te llamé Sochilt porque significa reina de flores en azteca y yo no escribí así porque hay muchas Xochitl pero sola una Sochilt."* From that day forward, having learned that my name meant Queen of the Flowers made me start to appreciate my Aztec name and realized that the way people say my name doesn't matter when you understand what it stands for.

Being raised in a Salvadoran household with a mom that only knew Spanish at the time meant every day consisted of Spanish. My cousins and other family members that I love dearly came over to enjoy good food, but they came over to gossip and socialize and bond and every conversation was in Spanish and everyone understood everyone. As a toddler, this wasn't a worry to me, and my mother and I would have conversations on the bus about our day and what we'd have for dinner. Once school started, I felt the world was so tiny and I was alone. "Don't speak Spanish" was a constant reminder in school. Being one of few kids who couldn't understand English, soon my Spanish was gone. Reading, writing, and speaking seemed like a challenge now, since I was focused on learning English so much.

With the help of some Spanish classes I slowly remembered my abilities to speak, write, and read in my native language. Looking back, I regret not taking learning Spanish seriously. Now that I'm older, I realize that Spanish made me more culturally wealthy because now when I'm in the car with my mother I'm able to enjoy conversations with her and I'm able to know that she understands me just as well as I understand her.

Wealth of Friends, Family, and Community

ETHAN Q. * *age 16*
John O'Connell High School

The community around me was small, but tightly knit. Everyone knew each other; neighbors became friends; friends became family. Belize was a unique country and their unique traditions reinforced that. Some of my favorite memories came from the holidays and traditions that they have. September was a month full of celebrations. I could vividly remember standing on my balcony and watching the color-filled celebrations of Carnival pass through the streets, or the patriotism of the Independence Day parade echo throughout the city. At midnight, fireworks would be shot into the dark night and explode with a bang before a rainbow of colors would shimmer and cascade into the night.

My friends and I share many fond memories, too. Every day during school or after school we'd sit at a table and have heated political discussions, laughter-filled commentary, or even juicy, gossip-filled exchanges. Some days we'd help each other with homework or study for a test. Other days we'd play cards or chess. All of these things made the school day more enjoyable, and it made me feel like I was a part of something. I had people that I could rely on and truly refer to as friends. They made me feel that I was part of a larger family, which was not related by blood, but instead by friendship. My family was also very important to me and were very supportive. We share many wonderful memories and traditions that have greatly influenced me.

Mud Fight

ANILU Z. * *age 13*
Everett Middle School

The bright sun tried to shine through the windows of our white living room, but failed once it reached the white shades. Even with the A/C on, the sauna-like outdoors could be felt by my six-year-old self.

"Kids! Come out here!" my father's hoarse voice yelled from outside. I wasn't allowed to go outside without my mother. She always gave me the feeling of safety, the way her soft hand shaped my hand. And plus it was a rule of hers. The aching feeling in my stomach told me that something was coming for us and it was urgent to obey my father's order.

My brother, Andrew, probably did some dumb teenage boy thing and now all our butts were going to be on our dad's wall. Countless ideas popped in and out of my head. The sweat started to pound down, one drop after the other, as I inched my way toward the scratched up door. My palms became so sweaty that when I went to turn the doorknob, it slipped.

"Move out the way!" Andrew shoved me out the way, and my small self flew back ten hundred feet and landed with an *oomp* on the hard tile floor of the kitchen. He flung the door open and ran outside. Before he could move from the door, gushes of water came flying toward him. Loud cries came from him as he marched over to my dad, who was on the other side of the yard, guilty with the hose in his hand.

Andrew's slumped body turned to alert and aggressive in a matter of seconds as his fists turned into balls. His legs pumped fast as he marched over to my father. Andrew's face was inches from my dad who was trying to hold in his laughter.

"No fighting!" I screamed as I ran across to the two males. Before I could make it there, my butt felt the nice, mushy ground. A hot watery feeling was caught in my eyes and things didn't work when my brother kept laughing at me.

My hands found a way to the ground and for a while I studied the thick substance I was sitting on. Just like with a snowball, I grabbed a handful of the mud and my small short arm moved perfectly in the direction toward my brother.

Game Winner

LEON M. * *age 13*
Everett Middle School

When I got picked up from my uncle, I was excited to go to my basketball game. I was thinking on the way there, *what can me and my team do to win this game?* I was thinking that we should play as a team and not play hero ball and play good defense. So when I got to the gym, our team got together and started warming up for three minutes. The warm-ups are two lines on the side with the ball and the other side without the ball. The side with the ball goes to shoot the ball, and the other line gets the ball, and you keep the rotation going. After that, the team started stretching. The stretches are high-knees, lunges, and karoakes. Then, our coach called us over and everybody was nervous. I knew it was my time to shine. I gave a pep talk and said, "Let's go and win this game!" Then I said, "Play hard, be tough, play together," and they all said it with me excitedly.

After I pumped up my teammates, we started to feel good about ourselves and knew that we were going to win this game. It was time for tip-off. I was jumping up and down proudly. Then we won the tip-off. When we were in the game it was tough, because the other team was good and really aggressive, so we had to do the same thing to win this game.

The score was 27–27 and we were playing good defense, but then my teammate fouled out and then one of the players got to shoot two free throws. He made the first shot and his team went crazy. He shot the second one, made it again, and the crowd went crazy.

It was a two-point game, three seconds left on the clock, and my teammate passed me the ball. I ran down the court and as I shot it from half court, the other team fouled me. The crowd was surprised and then I got to shoot three free throws. I was super nervous but I just had to let it go. When I was about to shoot my three free throws, the other team was booing me, but I just had to ignore them. The first shot went in and it was 28–29. Then I shot another one. It bounced around the rim, and it went in. Everybody went crazy. Now, it was 29–29. I shot my third free throw and I was not nervous because I knew I was going to make it. I bounced the ball two times, then stopped, shot, and it went in. The crowd went crazy and everybody was on the court.

Bike Life

ALEJANDRO C. * *age 16*
Downtown High School

On a late Sunday morning, a group of friends and I meet up at McLaren Park or a certain spot and wait for the pack to go say, "Wassup," to everyone, get ready, help unload bikes off the truck, and stuff like that. About thirty minutes or an hour or later, we start to ride out.

I hear people trying to talk over their engines with the hot sun making the bikes pop out. Sometimes we will go to Twin Peaks. Mid-ride on the way there, we hear the bike when the rider pops the clutch and the smell of gas.

When we get to Twin Peaks, it's more people to get to know. Even though we are around a bunch of people I don't know, it doesn't feel like they're strangers at all. It's like everyone there just has a positive energy toward each other. Even though we are all from different 'hoods, when we are all together, it's like we are all a big family from all races and ethnicities from every 'hood and city in the Bay Area. It's not something you see around here. It's a rare feeling and sight to us.

I met someone in my high school and we really didn't get along. One time in a ride-out, we saw each other and we just shook hands. Now we are really good friends, all because of some bikes.

This matters to me because I feel like it's something I'm actually good at and I feel like I'm actually a part of something.

I think if this kind of community didn't exist, I probably would still be getting in trouble and ending up in bad situations and stuff. This is a kind of escape for me. If I am feeling stressed or something, I just go out by myself or with a friend and just forget everything and clear up my head.

Brothers

BRIAN P. * *age 13*
Everett Middle School

When I get home I feel like I'm breaking the law. It's dead silent to the point where I can hear a fly fart. The TV is off and the couches look like they've never been touched before. The only light I have is the sleeping blue of the morning ready to be awakened. I take out my phone and see the crack on it, like the crack in my mind when I'm set off and I think subjectively instead of objectively. When I fight with my little brother, it never ends well.

Like when we got into a fight at Costco, I was thinking of only me and how unfair it was instead of how it affected my mom. My brother threw a cake at me and we got kicked out. We're cats and dogs, never giving up the chance to ruin each other's day.

My mother made lasagna yesterday and I saved some. Every bite feels like a nuclear bomb of flavor exploding in my mouth. After thirty seconds it feels like an eternity slowly crushing me. I'm craving the nutrition and flavor as I grab the magnum opus of the culinary arts, and it burns my hands like 10,000 wasps stinging my hands. So I sit anxiously with the heavenly aroma, but at the corner of my eye I see a gremlin-like shadow.

"Hey, Brian." It's my brother. His words send cold shivers down my spine, like a snake dancing around it. "Give me some," he continues.

"No," I say boldly, like a truck hitting him.

"Why not?" he says in a more serious tone.

"You had enough last night. Plus, you'll probably lose or drop it. You're not responsible," I say, taking a verbal stand.

What I Used to See

CHARVIERA A. * *age 17*
Burton High School

Walking out my door, I used to see old men playing cards. I used to see old women talking about the latest gossip. I used to hear the boys on dirt bikes racing down the streets. These are things I used to see and hear. I used to wake up in the morning to the sound of my neighbor's raspy voice yelling, "Don't park in front of my house!"

My neighbor Miss Jerry lived next to me for fourteen years. She wasn't the nicest person on the outside, but had a loving heart on the inside. I remember going over to her house when my mother couldn't pick me up for school. Her house was a warm, heated place that smelled of her dinner cooking in the oven. She would always slice me a piece of 7-Up cake and make me sit in the kitchen until my mom came.

One day, my mom got a call from her saying she had lost her house. She had fought to keep this house for years. She put all of her hard work into this house and it had just been taken like it was nothing. At first I really didn't understand why it was so bad that she had to move, until I realized the significance of her home. Her home was her pride and joy, her biggest accomplishment. The day she had to finally leave, I could see the pain and the feeling of disappointment in her face. I could see that she was disappointed with the fact that she had to let go so easily.

Since the day Miss Jerry left, I see sale signs and hear moving trucks coming in. People who grew up in my community have memories of spending hot days swimming at Martin Luther King Jr. Pool, memories of playing basketball with friends at Joe Lee Gym, and memories of going to the YMCA to do Zumba classes. These memories are slowly being taken away.

Medusa's Ride!

WISDOM O. * *age 13*
Everett Middle School

It took us around ten minutes to choose our first ride, and my brother said, "Let's ride the Medusa."

I replied, "No, that's the biggest ride here!"

But he said, "If you don't do it with me, you won't play *FIFA '17* for the rest of the year."

So I said, "Fine! Fine! I will do it." As we made it to the line for Medusa it was outrageously long. I was also outrageously scared for my life. The ride looked like a humongous green anaconda. I have been always scared of heights for my whole life. I remembered a time when I hiked up Bernal Heights last year and I almost slipped down. Medusa had a 150-foot drop, which was really scary. It took us around thirty minutes to finally get on. Before it was about to take its 150-foot-drop, I was literally crying. I was literally in tears. But my crying didn't help because I still did the ride. When I went down the 150-foot-drop, the wind blew my tears up. Also during the huge drop, my insides felt like they weren't there at all and I felt like I was floating.

Even though I was dizzy after getting off the ride, I was still happy that I conquered the biggest ride at Six Flags. I was delighted that I overcame my fear of heights. I felt like I had the courage to climb high distances.

Thirteen Years Old

SAMIRA R. ✳ *age 14*
Leadership High School

Thirteen is really hard. Everyone thinks that you can do everything your parents do, like cooking, cleaning clothes, or other stuff. But thirteen is just a number. It is actually about who you are, not what age. But any number is a day to be responsible, except for five and down.

When you are thirteen, you feel young, but at the same time old. This age is a feeling that you could be an adult when your parents aren't there for you or your siblings. Thirteen is the age when you can start helping people with stuff. The great thing about being thirteen is that when you were young you couldn't see PG-13 movies, but now that you're kind of old enough you can see them.

I think that our parents should give us a chance to speak our minds, so what I mean is: "Believe in me and let me have a chance to speak my own opinion."

My name feels like a summer breeze rolling off your tongue. The poems that follow are brimming with all kinds of different flavors; read them out loud and see how they taste. Some are sweet like mangos, some taste like spring flowers, and others are more like trickles of rain that show us what determination looks like. These odes to food, powerful haikus, and poems about names are bursting with zest and spice, so read on and enjoy. ✳

Bright as a Mango

Poetry

Walking from El Salvador

HILDA H. * *age 9*
Buena Vista Horace Mann

My family is special to me,
because they are like candy and the ocean.
I am from Eggo waffles,
and pizza because it is hot like the sun.

My home is special to me,
because it is like a flower.
My family is like the ocean,
and my dog is so, so big,
like the moon.

My home is very happy,
like when I eat candy.
It has blue, pink, black, and purple flowers,
and roses and big trees.

I am from Salvadoran food,
from *pupusas,*
and Texan food.
My grandma's name is Hilda,
and my family goes to the park,
because they love me.

My family is so funny,
and they are happy people.
When I was a child,
I was told to be kind and respectful,
and my family's favorite song is *"Despacito."*

I am from going out to eat for birthdays,
from Salvadoran food.
My family is important to me,
they are from El Salvador and Texas.

A story I was told was when my grandma came walking to
    San Francisco,
walking from El Salvador.

Soul of a Lion

KWAN B. * *age 14*
YCD Summer Bridge

I have the soul of a lion,
hear me roar.
I am a courageous warrior,
ready for war.
I fought tigers and bears,
including boars.
I'm proud to say my name is Kwan,
for I am the king of the lions,
the greatest one.
I'm on top of the world,
king of kings.
Stronger than any wave,
that's the lion soul in me.
I can never be beat.
They tremble at my feet,
but I'm a nice guy when you get to know me.

Butterflies in Mind

KEIAUNA M. ✳ *age 14*
Everett Middle School

Crazy like Jell-O
As hyper as a monkey
Heartbeat like hip-hop

Pizza Poem

JAKE G. * *age 16*
Mission High School

When I see a kitchen, I know.
Starting cooking, I will go.
Got to start from scratch,
making fresh food
because that's what makes it good.
My kitchen is my home,
pizza is from Rome.
I wonder who the first cook was?
I follow as he does.

All tasty and round,
don't drop it on the ground.

Smell that cheese,
got me hungry.
Now I'm happy.

Bliss

DIEGO V. ✷ *age 14*
Everett Middle School

Strolling through nature
A newfound peace inside me
Redwoods standing tall

In Amor with Horror

MEYBELIN M. * *age 18*
Mission High School

Scary movies, you are my favorite addiction.
What would I do without you and the adrenaline that I feel
    when something bad is going to happen?

You are the reason I don't go to the bathroom at night.
You make me run from the darkness so fast that you can't
    see my feet.
You are the reason why I never play with dolls.

When I watch you, my heart beats so fast and my stomach
    flip-flops.
But I can't pause you. I spend all my money and time to be
    with you.

Just you and me, and my eyes burning. I love you so much
    that I don't mind living my life with the light on at night.

I go back to you because your mystery is my weakness.
Even though you make me scream,
and people think that I'm scared when I'm really not,
I want more and more of you.

What Does Sadness Look Like?

JOANNA H. ✳ *age 13*
Theodore Roosevelt Middle School

Im fine im fine
Im fine im fine im fine
Im fine im fine im fine im fine
Im fine im fine im fine im fine im
fine im fine im fine im fine im fine
fine im fine im fine im fine im fine im
fine im fine im fine im fine im fine im
fine im fine im fine im fine im fine im
im fine im fine im fine im fine im   *no really*
fine im fine im fine im fine im fine   *im fine im okay*
fine im fine im fine im fine im
im fine im fine im fine im
fine im fine im fine im fine im fine im
Im fine im fine im fine im fine im fine im fine
Im fine im fine im fine im fine im fine im fine im
fine im fine im fine im fine im fine im fine im fine
Help me help me help me help me help me help me
Help me help me help me help me help me help me
Help me help me help me help me help me help me
Help me help me help me help me help me help me

The Brown Violin

EVELIN D. * *age 14*
Everett Middle School

The music sound waves
Colorful like the spring air
Is all I can see

A Mexican Am I, No One Can Stop Me

BRANDON R. ✱ *age 14*
Everett Middle School

My hair, black like night,
my skin, dark-tan, like the sand.
I am Mexican.

Strength in Me

MYRAI M. ✳ *age 14*
Everett Middle School

I'm a strong black girl.
Despite the stereotypes,
I know my true strength.

The "Gift"

NALA T. ✳ *age 13*
YCD Summer Bridge

My name means "gift."
You can either open the present or give it away.
My name sounds like a lion in the thunderstorm,
but feels like the summer breeze rolling off your tongue.
My name is like the color red because when you see me,
    that's all you see.
They say my name is Nayla, but it's Nala,
but it doesn't really bother me
because I'm used to it.
I am Lil' Simba,
not just joyful and fun, but wild and fearless with
    no regrets.
I have tough skin like an onion.
You just have to deal with me one layer at a time.
My name fits me . . . unique and wild.

Midfielder

JAYDON L. * *age 14*
Everett Middle School

Cold rain on my face,
my mind races to keep up,
determined to win.

Burritos and Me

AIRIAS D. ✳ *age 16*
Mission High School

Oh burritos,
you make me feel
like there is nothing else in the world.
The way you slide down,
down into my stomach,
it's like you are filling a void in my body.

Like a swimming pool on a hot day,
all of your ingredients are swimming inside me.
Nothing cures me like you do, burritos.
It's like I was under a curse,
and when I eat you, the curse has been lifted.

When the world is too much for me,
I can just get a burrito.

It is like you just make time stop,
take all of my problems away,
when me and you meet together,
face to face.

It's just like I am almost in heaven,
and your melty cheese is so good, like lava.

I Am as Bright as a Mango

DAEJAH C. * *age 17*
Mission High School

I'm like that sweet, yellow, juicy mango
you taste, after you peel it.
I'm learning the growth
out of childhood life,
on to adulthood.

I'm hard, risky, for anything necessary.
I'm worth it, so worth it,
because on the inside I'm soft.
Softer than butter.

I'm fresh, but can get slippery.
I'm all you need
on a bright, sunny summer day.
But one thing's for sure,
I can be a pricey one.

I'm joyful and
extremely good
for your health.

The Enmity and Entity of a Basketball

ZACH E. ∗ *age 15*
Ruth Asawa School of the Arts

Let's get one thing straight:
I am a basketball, "and it's my favorite sport,"
"I wish I was a baller," they dribble me up and down the court.
But I feel exploited:
they caress my leather-flesh then bludgeon me into a net.
I'm utilized physically; they think I'm a pet.
I feel invigorated, innovated,
shot up in an arc, so when I swish they say,
"It's in, I made it!"
I revel in it, but I also feel ambivalent.
You can call me cavalier,
not from Cleveland,
but I'm the "rock" that they're seein', but
I've underwent through spurts of runs, splashes
that have hurt amongst the repugnant perspiration
of sweaty, cotton t-shirts at the Y.
I ask myself, "Why?" every day,
but something about players shooting, bellowing,
"ALL DAY!"

I am a basketball, but I love it.
I am always regulated
like a puppet.
Teams fabricate their offense off of me,
but it's exciting when I watch some quality
like the Dubs
I'm in awe.
Ostentatiously, they play preeminently,
heavily passing, opaque cutting, or defending thee.
They dropping dimes,
as if I was a spending spree.
Mentally,
I'm beloved at the playground.
Ricochet, "in yo' face," I'm a rebound.
Steal me, dunk it, or penetrate to the rack.
I'm omnipotent, they're into it
and that's a fact.

So Imma leave while I exit—
nah, I'm just kidding, "I'm back."
Like what Steph said in game four:
"Trailblazing" the track.
Seventeen in only five still leading
the pack.
I smack, compact, extract, flipping, spinning
intact.
I get passed or outletted to be laid in
the sack.
That sack of fiber net ripped and swished
'til it cracks.
I get bounced and rolled 'til they're satisfied.
I'm shot up in the air
'til I get buried inside.
The gravity I defy in the sky flying high,
but descending straight down while
y'all look with your eyes.

So cherish I, but I'll still perish
and die.
Until you pump me back up, pressurized
with a needle, test the air while you
can so I can't get popped from a
beetle.
I get annoyed from bad play,
like Patrick Star yelling
"Leedle!"
So use me right—not out of spite—
I'm not Evel Knievel.

So don't abuse me I tire, too,
and I'll fatigue
'til I'm
feeble.
Just remember,
I'm a basketball,
I got power,
I'm lethal.

At its best, journalism is an expression of empathy. Tackling everything from immigration policy, the continuing fight for LGBTQ+ inclusion, and the dangers of black holes, these articles ask us to pause and pay attention to overlooked issues. True humanity means listening to others' stories and expressing the compassion shown in these pages. ✳

True Humanity Means We're All Important

Journalism

The Search for the American Dream

HENDDEL C. * *age 19*
Mission High School

Immigrants say they come to United States for a better life. But this means different things for different people. Some come for a better education for themselves and for their children. They come to work to support their families. They also come to escape the violence in their countries.

My mother said she came to the United States from Mexico because of poverty and to find a job to support me and my brothers. It was difficult to find a job in her village. "I came for the American Dream," my mother told me. She worked full time to earn money to send to me and my brothers one or two times a month. My mother said, "I worked a lot of hours to save money and send it to Mexico . . . I only planned to stay for two years, but I stayed longer because I needed to pay for the house I had in San Luis Potosi." She earned enough money to bring me, my brother, and my sister to America.

According to the Public Policy Institute of California, 6% of California's population is undocumented immigrants. And Pew Research Center reports 9% of California's workforce are undocumented immigrants. This shows that undocumented immigrants work more than people who are citizens, and that most come to California with the objective of working.

Another reason that immigrants come here is to escape violence in their home countries and make new lives. According to the U.S. Department of Homeland Security, "155,000 children have crossed the southern border alone in the last three years, the majority of them fleeing violent gangs, poverty, and domestic abuse in El Salvador, Guatemala, and Honduras."

Mission Magazine talked to three seventeen-year-old students from International High School in San Francisco, who just came here from Guatemala. We asked them why they came to America. "A better life," they all said.

"Did you experience violence in Guatemala?" we asked.

"All of us," one of them said. The other two nodded. "In my village, twelve-year-olds were joining gangs."

In a recent article in the *Huffington Post*, Roque Planas wrote, "The conventional wisdom says that most Latin American migrants who come to the United States are looking for a better life, inspired by the 'American Dream.' And it's hard to deny that there's a lot of truth in that. But there's another side to the story—people leave Latin America because life there can be very hard. Poverty, political instability, and recurring financial crises often conspire to make Latin American life more challenging than in the U.S., a wealthy country with lots of job opportunities."

It's important for American citizens to understand that immigrants come here for good reasons. I know the reasons because I am an immigrant who came to have a new life with opportunities in a new society. I came here with the same ideas as others. The American Dream is something every immigrant has in mind. We know life here is not easy. But I know that immigrants won't give up because they're moving closer to their dreams.

Why Is Trump Afraid of Kittens? Trump Threatens Free Speech Online

SKYLAR L. * *age 8*
Children's Day School

Kittens scare President Trump. Don't believe me? Listen to what seventeen-year-old Lucy has to say. After Lucy built the website *Kittenfeed.com*, which uses kitten paws to punch President Trump, she received a cease-and-desist and legal action claim from Trump's lawyers. "It's so sad that his administration is focused more on being liked, burying real news, and taking down sites like mine as they supposedly make him look bad," she said.

I've been on *Kittenfeed.com*, and while it is a strange site, I am still surprised that Trump felt a need to go after Lucy. According to an article by Sage Lazzaro of the *Observer*, "Lucy is a seventeen-year-old from San Francisco who spends her spare time reading at coffee shops, splurging on guac at Chipotle, and practicing her tech skills."

A local news station, PIX 11, reported an interview with Nicholas Fortuna, a corporate litigator who stated that,

"Freedom of speech gives anyone the right to criticize and even make fun of the president, even if it's with kitten paws."

The article additionally says that Trump's grounds for the cease-and-desist is based on a "trademark infringement" claim. However, Fortuna believes that Trump is wrong.

I decided to talk to Jennifer Lin, a lawyer, to ask more about free speech online and why it's important. "It's important because it's tempting for certain political figures to silence speech they don't like. Trump's trademark claim is a pretty transparent attempt to limit speech," says Lin.

Lucy getting the attention of the President of the United States even though she is only a seventeen-year-old wanting to learn to code shows why free speech is important and also powerful. I think that free speech is important because it is harmful to the president.

Save the Penguins, Save Ourselves

JACORE B. ✳ *age 11*
Homeschool

Why should kids care about global warming? How will global warming affect us? How does what we do affect global warming? And how do we fix it?

Over the past 200 years, the earth has been getting warmer because of pollution. Greenhouse gases have caused the temperature near the surface of the earth to increase.

"As the earth warms, more of the ocean's water goes into the atmosphere and disrupts the normal weather patterns," says Tracy Zhu, a former environmental fellow at the San Francisco Foundation and an analyst at the Public Utilities Commission. "Places that normally experience rain storms would get more severe storms, or perhaps get no storms at all. Places that are normally dry may get even drier . . . The balance of the earth is thrown off with climate change."

Global warming is bad for the earth. When the earth gets warmer, it starts making severe weather on land and the sea. As global warming gets worse, the polar ice caps melt more and more with each passing day. The melting of the polar ice caps affects life in the poles, which could eventually mean no more penguins, polar bears, or walruses. This month, scientists discovered that a crack in the Antarctic ice shelf grew by seventeen miles in two months. Antarctica holds nearly 90% of the word's ice mass.

But how does it affect people? According to the National Oceanic and Aeronautic Association, about 97% of the earth's water is salt water. The other 3% is stored in lakes and rivers underground—and in our glaciers, which are disappearing. We can try removing the salt from the ocean water, but according to the Texas Water Development Board, desalination costs "approximately 658 million dollars to build a seawater desalination plant." It's not worth it!

How do humans contribute to global warming? All the gases and fumes from processing plants and vehicles get stuck in the atmosphere. The sunrays go through the earth's atmosphere but not out, and that heats up the earth. Cows also make the earth heat up. In fact, according to the United Nations, raising cattle puts more greenhouse gases into the atmosphere than cars—almost 18% of global releases.

So how do we fix it? According to Zhu, the damage done so far is irreversible. But we can make changes for the future. "Changes we make now, such as burning fewer fossil fuels, will have impacts thirty to forty years from now," Zhu says. To do your part, the Environmental Protection Agency suggests you can use your water more efficiently, conserve power, be green in your yards, and reduce, reuse, and recycle.

Meet Gabby Douglas, the Woman Who Is Inspiring Me to Go into Gymnastics

TATIANA O. * *age 9*
César Chavéz Elementary School

I am trying to be on a gymnastics team and I can do the splits and a handstand underwater. That is why I am starting to do sit-ups and push-ups, too. My report is about Gabby Douglas. Who is Douglas? She is a gymnast and she does a lot of flips, including flips on the beam! She is famous for winning gold medals in the Olympics.

Douglas knew she wanted to be a gymnast when she was really young and she was watching her sister practice. When I interviewed Douglas she said, "My older sister Arielle, who was a gymnast, taught me my first gymnastics skills. I started off doing cartwheels and round-offs." Her mom enrolled her in classes soon after.

Training for the Olympics is hard, and Douglas would know since she has been there. "I trained for two years before the Rio Olympics," she says. She would wake up at 7:00 a.m. to start training at 8:00 a.m. every day. Her training was very hard, and she would do things like practice her floor routine, practice vaults, beam, and even climb a twelve-foot rope with no legs! The training paid off, because she won three Olympic medals.

Finally, the last important part is that Douglas is not training right now. She says, "Right now, I am enjoying spending time with my family. I'm also able to experience some pretty amazing opportunities, too!" Douglas is a great person and she trains really hard. She is exciting and very beautiful and she makes me happy. I hope to be as good as her one day!

The Ivory Trade

GENEVIEVE B. * *age 11*
Everett Middle School

Have you ever thought of the adorable elephants in Asia and Africa and how they're doing? Well, if you think "good" then you're definitely wrong. About fifty-five elephants are being killed per day (about 20,075 elephants per year). This is all because of the ivory trade, and how people mis-sell their ivory.

Because of frontline enforcement and political support, poaching has dropped to pre-2008 levels. John Scanlon, General Secretary of the Convention on International Trade in Endangered Species, said, "Eastern Africa has been badly affected by the surge in poaching over the last ten years and has experienced an almost 50% reduction in its elephant population." He continued, "There has, however, been a steady decline in poaching levels since its peak in 2011, and the analysis from 2016 concludes that overall poaching trends have now dropped to pre-2008 levels. This shows us what is possible through sustained and collective frontline enforcement and demand reduction efforts, coupled with strong political support."

You may still wonder what ivory is, and why poachers need and want it. Innocent elephants are killed by poachers for their ivory, which is removed from the tusks of the elephant. Ivory is used for decoration and, for example, in China, people in higher classes use ivory as a status symbol, and ivory chopsticks, jewelry, carvings, etc. are used to show off wealth. Ivory also can be sold for a lot, so this is why so many elephants are killed per year!

Elephants are becoming extinct because of this, and just think about how many more elephants there would be if we didn't kill any last year. There would be about an extra 20,000 elephants! This is a really big problem to me and many others because elephants and so many other animals are a very large part of the food chain. Get it? Well, this is another reason. I think many big and popular ivory factories are closing. But I also know someone who can help.

The San Francisco Zoo is only one S.F. organization that you could look into to help stop the ivory trade. They even researched the ivory trade, and at the beginning of 2017, about ninety-nine elephants were being killed per day for their ivory.

Overall, I think the illegal ivory trade is a horrible event in history because of how ivory is mis-sold. Also 20,075 innocent elephants are killed per year and a huge part of the food cycle is becoming endangered because of poachers. Remember, if you'd like to help save innocent elephants' lives, I recommend donating to charities or researching the topic to do what you can to help.

What You Might Not Know about Carrie Fisher

DIANA R. * *age 10*
Alvarado Elementary School

A lot of people know Carrie Fisher as Princess Leia, but what they might not know is that she also played many other characters. She was a celebrated author, playwright, and screenwriter. When Fisher died on December 27, 2016, at age sixty, many people learned more about her. After she died, I wanted to learn more about her.

Fisher started acting when she was fifteen, in 1975. She performed with her mother, actress Debbie Reynolds, on Broadway. Just two years later, she became world famous when she first appeared as Princess Leia in Star Wars. Fisher continued to act until her death, but over the years she also became known as a writer.

Not everyone knows how she became an actress and an icon for so many people.

Carrie Fisher was picked for Princess Leia because she was unique. She had something special that no one else had.

Fisher was willing to challenge herself. She really meant what she said. The director George Lucas thought that she would suit the character with her intelligence and sense of humor. He said her confidence made her special.

Tony Taccone, who directed Carrie Fisher in her one-woman show, *Wishful Drinking*, got to know her later in her career, and learned a lot of things about her. He agreed that her confidence and work was limitless.

"She loved the audience—the audience respected her, and she was an icon for many people. She meant something to them because she stood for openness and honesty, especially around her mental illness and issues of body-shaming. She stood up against harmful perceptions and images," said Taccone.

That's why Carrie Fisher went so far. She became more than an actress and a leader. She was inspiring on stage and on screen. But in her life off-screen she was even more inspiring. She was a voice for people that needed her. She'll always be remembered for that.

"She was willing to speak out," said Taccone. "People loved her for that."

Should We Be Afraid of Black Holes?

LAURENCE G. * *age 12*
Benjamin Franklin Middle School

Have you ever wondered what a black hole is and what's inside of it? Do you think that we are already in a black hole, full of darkness? How powerful are black holes? Could it even be a portal to an even bigger universe or galaxy distant from us? According to NASA, "A black hole is a place in space where gravity pulls so much that even light cannot get out. The gravity is so strong because matter has been squeezed into a tiny space. This can happen when a star is dying." This can create a background on how black holes work and how powerful they are. Black holes are formed when a star dies, which is called a supernova.

Black holes are one of the strangest things in the universe, and not much is known about them. They come in many sizes and masses. For example, a supermassive black hole at the center of our galaxy called NGC 5195 has the mass of an estimated twenty-billion suns! According to NASA, "Stellar black holes form when the center of a very massive star collapses in upon itself. This collapse also causes a supernova, or an exploding star, that blasts part of the star into space. The size of the supermassive black hole is related to the size and mass of the galaxy it is in." Just imagine if you were about 1,000 kilometers away from one of these massive black holes.

Black holes are so powerful that even light can't escape, and light can travel for 187,000 miles per second! In order to escape though, you would have to be faster than this, which isn't possible for you, anyone else, or any piece of matter in this universe, yet. However, how are black holes able to do this? According to *Space.com*, "Black holes are incredibly massive, but cover only a small region. Because of the relationship between mass and gravity, this means they have an extremely powerful gravitational force. Virtually nothing can escape from them—under classical physics, even light is trapped by a black hole." This shows how powerful a black hole can be. Recently, five separate black holes were seen from a highly advanced telescope, which were all merging into one super massive black hole.

According to *Seekandsource.com*, "There is a theory that within a black hole there's something called a singularity. A singularity is what all the matter in a black hole gets crushed into. Some people talk about it as a point of infinite density at the center of the black hole, but that's probably wrong— true, it's what classical physics tells us is there, but the singularity is also where classical physics breaks down, so we shouldn't trust what it says here." Imagine yourself, about 500 miles from one of these things. Would you survive? Even if you said "yes," I highly doubt your chances of survival. However, we don't know everything about black holes because of how strange they are. If we did know everything about black holes, then we would be able to answer if they're portals to another galaxy or universe, and how to destroy them.

In conclusion, black holes can be one of your biggest fears in space because of how even light can't escape them. No one or thing in this universe can escape them because of how strong their gravitational pull is. In my opinion, if one was approximately one to two light years away (which is 11.4 trillion miles away) and heading right toward us, then I would do everything I would like to do before it comes and devours us all.

The Ladder of Thorns for Muslims and Undocumented People in a Luxurious Palace (the U.S.)

MOHAMMED K. ✳ *age 19*
Mission High School

The real and harsh truth of living in the United States is getting targeted because of your religion or ethnicity. The blatant bigotry of President Trump makes Muslims and undocumented people feel guilty for having that background.

The U.S. has a very large number of people who are from different countries all over the world. Sadly, many of them are undocumented because they do not have green cards or legal citizenship. Even worse is Trump's presidency and his policies because he has vowed to build a wall on Mexico's border (the root of the illegal entrance). Despite being undocumented, these people's perseverance and hard work in every field makes this country beautiful and great. However, these people don't get the opportunities they want because they aren't eligible due to their immigration status.

A lot of people feel hopeless in this current environment. Muslims may feel it the worst. "The worst feeling of being segregated has just recently been felt by me because of the temporary ban executed by our president, Donald Trump," said Salah. Salah is a student at Mission High School from Yemen, one of the six countries Trump has banned. Salah and his siblings became naturalized citizens of the U.S. because they were under the age of eighteen, and their father was already a legal citizen and has stayed in the U.S. for about thirty years.

A different friend of mine has been living in the U.S. for almost four years now. Being undocumented, he feels restricted from opportunities and from the love our community has for documented immigrants. The major issue for him and his family is to survive through their situation with no support other than their own perseverance. Being a high school student, my friend works four days a week for seven hours each day, which really prevents him from getting adequate rest or finishing his school work. In addition to that, he is often frightened about running into any sort of police, who are known for deporting large groups of undocumented people, and about getting targeted by Trump's policies.

All these problems get worse for Muslim people, especially those from predominantly Muslim countries. The society has sharp eyes on Muslims by suspecting them as terrorists or as being harmful to the country. My friend Salah's case is typical. Salah said that he and his family already knew that Trump was racist and bigoted, specifically toward Arabs and Muslims.

"My family wanted to support the people who were protesting by joining their rallies," Salah said. "My presence in protests made them satisfied. Since we are all citizens of the U.S., my family led me to stay calm and feel free to travel. Also, my rights as a citizen make me equal to citizens of any other race or religion. I felt very proud when I saw people of color, LGBTQ people, and white people protesting together to resist the ban on people from all of the banned countries."

But other Muslims feel insecure and directly targeted because of the president's thinking and hate toward them. They feel fearful of being Muslims and hopeless since there is no one who can guarantee them the ability to stay and make their futures better. The reason why most Muslims move is not terrorism, but the search for a healthy and prosperous life in a wealthy and united country.

As an Indian Muslim, I live freely and happily, but my family advises me to stay safe and not stay out late at night because of my skin color. Often times people recognize me as a Latino and treat me based on my appearance. So, the overall conclusion is that Muslims all over the world are being oppressed and are treated unequally because of their religion and their clothing. And undocumented immigrants in the U.S. have not yet gotten full rights and opportunities and their quandaries are only increasing because of people like Donald Trump. True humanity does not mean seeing or making any person feel less important just because of any kind of comparison between them and other people. The mentality of a leader who believes he deserves the best in the world should not take away the rights of others.

Latinas! How They Are Dealing with School and Work

MARIA S. ✳ *14*
Everett Middle School

When you're at school, do you realize you may have the upper hand in your education because of your race? If so, you might not notice that people underestimate you based on the following: race, education, and potential jobs.

In colleges from 1990 to 1998, the gap between Latinos and white people became clearer than before. According to the article, "Mexican Americans and Other Latinos in Postsecondary Education," on *Ericdigests.org*, "In 1998, while white, non-Latino college participation rate was 67.3%, the calculated rate for Latinos was 47.5%, the lowest rate since 1990." This shows how white and non-Latino colleges were more successful and had a higher percentage of people who attended classes. This is important because it shows that again, the dominant race in education was white people and the less dominant, or oppressed race, was Latinos.

For Latinos, finding high-paying jobs, for the most part, is very difficult. According to an article called "New Job Opportunities for Hispanics/Latinos," found on *Monster.com*, "Hispanics/Latinos find new paths to higher paying careers, yet Hispanics/Latinos accounted for 41% of maids and house-keepers." This conveys that even if Latinos find new ways to obtain high-paying jobs, still about 41% are maids or house-keepers. This statistic is crucial to understand because it shows that many Latinos can't get the same jobs as people of other races. The education they may or may not have received is connected to why they might not have higher paying jobs.

Throughout the years, many things have changed. Now the Latino population has grown. Now 5% of nurses are Latino, whereas before it was rarer to find a Latino with such a high paying job. This demonstrates that more Latinos are being recognized in the community. Now more than ever, our country needs the support of bilingual speakers, hence the growing demand for Latinos in high-paying jobs.

We Need Bilingual Education Again

KEVIN P. ✳ *age 18*
Mission High School

Until 1998, non-English speaking students in California could take classes in their own languages. Then, voters passed Proposition 227, which changed everything.

According to Edward Sifuentes, staff writer of *the San Diego Union-Tribune*, "Proposition 227 required that non-English-speaking students be placed in special one-year classes where instruction must be overwhelmingly in English, except with a written request from parents." The law meant that English learners had more struggles with English. It also deprived them of the vital skills of learning other subjects in their native language.

"Millions of Spanish-speaking immigrant students lost the opportunity to learn or retain valuable literacy skills in Spanish while they acquired English," wrote Phillip M. Carter for CNN. "And millions of California-born Latinos who enrolled in school with the gift of native bilingualism would later leave school unable to read and write in Spanish."

Many experts agree that bilingual education is a better way to learn. "When schools provide children quality education in their primary language, they give them two things: knowledge and literacy. The knowledge that children get through their first language helps make the English they hear and read more comprehensible," said Stephen Krashen, Professor Emeritus at the University of Southern California, who specializes in bilingual education.

At Mission High School, this bilingual education is necessary for newcomers who couldn't have the right to education in their homelands. "Bilingual education contributes to the developing of the brain and it makes us more efficient in daily tasks," said Ms. Rodriguez, a bilingual teacher in Mission High School. "This [bilingual] education is necessary to those who had a poor education in their countries. When they come here it is difficult for them to learn in another language that is not theirs."

Since we can't have a real bilingual education at Mission High School, we have programs that support newcomer students. For example, we have English Language Development (ELD) classes, and clubs like the *Organización Latina Estudiantil* (OLE), which help students take a break from the daunting English language and make them feel at home with Spanish speakers.

Personally, I think that bilingual education should return as a real bilingual education program, not only with small programs in some high schools with a low level of knowledge on the subjects. This type of education offers the benefits of bilingualism, like giving students access to current jobs where more than two languages are spoken, the freedom to travel around the world without the worry of knowing the native language of those places, and much more.

The Lego Loop

JULIAN R. * *age 11*
Everett Middle School

Lego is a popular interlocking brick system and with upcoming Lego movies, it doesn't seem like they are stopping any time soon. Besides going near to bankrupt in the early 2000s, still to this day Lego is up there as one of the biggest toy companies of all time. From a mother of two to a ten-year-old kid, nearly everyone has opened up a Lego set. But you most likely didn't know they started up as a small toy company in Denmark. It was about sixty years ago when Ole Kirk Christiansen bought the first plastic injection molding machine in Denmark. He wasn't the first person to use the molding machine, but he might well be the first person to make the brick so iconic.

Lego might have had a few ups and downs at the start, but the brand really took off when Christiansen bought his first molding machine at a toy convention. Before the iconic plastic bricks, the brand Lego started off with classic wooden toys. Then the brand went from wooden toys to plastic ones in the 1960s. But in 1993, sales started to go down, according to the movie *A Lego Brickumentary*, released on July 31, 2015. Then the company started to recover in 2004. But Legos aren't just toys for kids. In fact, there are channels on the platform YouTube from people like Jangbricks to Just2good who review

Lego sets. Also a lot of the YouTubers do some Lego MOCs, which is when you make your own creations.

I decided to take a survey to see what people think when they hear the word "Lego." Almost half of the people said they think of the colorful bricks, which goes to show how much people love the iconic brick. Does this sound familiar? You walk into your room and you take one big step, which might have been the worst mistake of your life. You look down and notice that you've stepped on a big pile of Legos. Some people I surveyed had this experience.

Since you can build almost anything out of Lego, it leads to a ginormous fan base. From a mother of two to a ten-year-old kid, nearly everyone has opened a Lego set. Since Lego has been around for years, multiple generations have had the opportunity to use it. Lego has become an icon for most generations.

Do You Want to Know More about Slime?

LISETTE L. ✳ *age 11*
César Chavéz Elementary School

Slime is made in different ways. There is butter slime and fluffy slime. The first slime is glue, water, and borax. A YouTube star from the channel *Will It Slime?*, whose real name is Adam, said, "I realized that slime was becoming popular on Instagram last year, but it had not yet exploded on YouTube. I saw an opportunity for growth on YouTube and created *Will It Slime?*.

Will It Slime? became so popular that it's now a full-time job. Adam says he spends about thirty hours a week testing new recipes and filming for YouTube now. "I am very happy making slime videos. It gives me more time to spend with my family and allows me to connect with fans around the world," he says.

I also emailed another slimey YouTube star, whose channel is called *Just Ameerah*. "It's super fun to experiment and put random stuff in slime," she told me. "Slime ideas just happen when I mix a bunch of random ingredients in slime, so I'm always trying to find a new slime."

I go to César Chavéz Elementary School where slime is banned, but some kids bring it to class. "I don't think schools should ban slime because I think slime is really relaxing, and when I'm reading a book or doing hands-free homework I like to poke slime because it helps me focus," said Ameerah. "I think schools are banning slime because kids could accidentally drop the slime or have their slime spill in their bag and it would create a sticky mess."

"I can understand why schools might ban slime if it is a distraction," said Adam. "Slime is awesome, but school is very important. Everyone should always strive to learn as much as they can. It's kind of funny though when I think about it because I actually learned how to make slime in science class."

I think slime is so cool to play with and you should try it!

What Will Happen to Undocumented Students?

JORGE C. * *age 14*
Everett Middle School

Those who have protection under Deferred Action for Childhood Arrivals (DACA) are worried about President Trump's next steps because he has said that he wants to repeal DACA. He declared he would only deport immigrants with criminal records, but the reality is that he is also deporting people who haven't committed crimes.

DACA is an executive permit passed by President Obama in 2012. The permit gives benefits to undocumented youth, allowing them to work and go to school in the United States. Nadia, a recipient of DACA, has lived in the U.S. since she was young. She received the permit in 2013, at age eighteen. She now fears the new administration will take away her permit and deport her. She has heard of five other undocumented youth protected under DACA being detained by Immigration and Customs Enforcement (ICE). The organization ThinkProgress states there are 730,000 undocumented youth being protected under DACA. If DACA is repealed, they will not have the means to work or go to school. Sean Spicer of Trump's administration says, "People who are in this country and pose a threat to public safety or have committed a crime will be the first to go and we will be aggressively making sure that they are first to go." While Spicer is saying that only criminals will get deported, only a million undocumented immigrants fit that criteria and Trump's administration also claims that anyone can be detained by ICE.

DACA is a permit that gives youth the opportunity to achieve the American Dream. This dream may become unreachable if the Trump administration decides to repeal the permit and deport the youth who only aspire to live better lives in a new country.

The Magic of Books

ANDREA A. * *age 10*
Thomas Edison Charter Academy

Do you think people watch more movies or read more books? Well, it's not even close. Americans watch five movies a year on average, according to a survey by Harris Interactive. But 23% of Americans didn't read even one book!

A good book should always be interesting and fun. Once you start a book you really like, you feel like you are living inside it. "When I pick a book, I want to escape," said Andrea Minarcek, an avid reader and a newspaper editor. I think books are magical because it is like having a movie in your head. But books aren't always magical for you, and it's not always easy to know if they are interesting before you buy or borrow them.

When you choose a book you say, "Which one should I choose?" Part of the reason it's hard is because there are so many books to choose from. In 2010, over three million books were published in the U.S., according to the *Huffington Post*.

One way a book is good is it has interesting characters. "I think strong characters make the best books," says Minarcek. "When I think of my favorite book, I don't think about the plot so much. I think about the characters as my friends."

If you don't like to read, try to find a book that looks interesting and it could change your mind. Open your mind to the world of books.

We Are Queer, We Have Been Here

MARVIN M. * *age 18*
Mission High School

The LGBTQ+ community in San Francisco and its struggles and stories have made San Francisco what it is. Chirtra Ramaswany once stated that "It is at once a celebration, an exercise in visibility and a timely reminder of how recently the battles for gay rights were won and how fragile those rights remain." The fight for equality and acceptance in S.F. is not over. There is still hope and we create that when we come together.

San Francisco has had a long history in LGBTQ+ rights. Rebellions, fights, strikes, and rallies were tactics that the LGBTQ+ community and allies have used to come together and overthrow the government. Compton Cafeteria was a safe space for trans people and gay men to meet. In August 1966, in the evening, the police interrupted the peace and started beating trans individuals for being part of the LGBTQ+ community. People started fighting back against police brutality and the harassment of this community, especially trans women. This rebellion acknowledges the fight that the LGBTQ+ community had to go through in order to contribute to Queer Stories.

Mission High School is a school close to the Castro District of San Francisco, well known as the gayest neighborhood in the country and where a lot of activism takes place. Teachers like Taica Hsu have been making sure that students have a safe space, like the Queer Student Alliance (QSA). I interviewed Taica, a math teacher at Mission High who also provides the space for the Queer Student Alliance, the only active LGBTQ+ group at Mission, and I asked him questions about the group. He said, "Eleven years ago, when I started working at Mission High, I heard that there was a QSA, but it was not very active." The Queer Student Alliance is a group run by students that makes sure that students meet other LGBTQ+ students to make the school a safer environment. Today around twenty-five students are involved in the group. Mission High School is the first and only school that hosts a colorful drag show, which creates visibility for queer students at Mission. It also educates the audience to become more aware of the community at Mission. According to Hsu, "The group helps students grow with their own identity, especially students who are new to the school. It helps the members find allies, and most important, it creates a safe space not just in classrooms, but in the hallways, and the school."

Being a member of this group has impacted a lot of students. For example, students become more open about their identity. In fact, a lot of students who were part of this group become community leaders, like Rexy Aramal, a Mission alumnus who creates change in California by working with LGBTQ+ students around Northern California. According to *the San Francisco Examiner*, "She joined Transform California, a new statewide campaign to ensure that all people can live safely, happily, and free from discrimination—whether that's at school, in the workplace, or in our communities."

In my role as president of the QSA, I have shown leadership by standing up for the LGBTQ+ community. I have conducted teach-ins in other classes at my school, covering topics such as gender-neutral pronouns and the importance of implementing gender neutral bathrooms at our school and district-wide. Additionally, during the spring we hosted our annual drag show. It was an amazing and colorful event. This created visibility and awareness for LGBTQ+ students at our school. Every year we have a political theme. For example, last year's theme was "Unity." Through my leadership, the QSA had an opportunity to meet with the administration of our school. We discussed issues such as the absence of mandated LGBTQ+ curriculum in the classroom at my school and district-wide and how my school could be more inclusive and friendly to queer students. The results from my efforts meeting with the principal and teachers were the following: the institution of LGBTQ+ curriculum in the classroom, students having access to a gender-neutral bathroom, and teach-ins on LGBTQ+ issues. Currently, in my role as president, I am focused on teaching lowerclassmen to continue the legacy of activism, social awareness, and LGBTQ+ visibility at Mission High School.

Mission High School has been working hard to make sure that students feel welcome and safe. In 2016, Jen Bowman, a social studies teacher at Mission High School, started the LGBTQ+ studies class, which serves to empower LGBTQ+ students as well as their allies. The curriculum is based on queer stories, learning about leaders in the community, different identities in the United States and the outside world, about gender and power and many more topics. A few years before, we also had activists come visit, like Pablo Rodriguez, a Two-Spirit person. (Two-Spirit people are indigenous peoples of the Americas who are very sacred and who do not fall into the gender binary.) Pablo is also an alumnus of Mission High School who helped organize the drag show at Mission. They were also part of the QSA and they took a lot of leadership in making Mission a better place for undocumented LGBTQ+ students. They also facilitated internships at Lavender Youth Recreation and Information Center

(LYRIC), a non-profit organization that builds communities and inspires them through social change.

These people have made Mission High School a safe and welcoming environment for LGBTQ+ students. Teachers and students at Mission have been building communities through social justice. Now it is our job to keep their vision going for the next generations of Mission students. People could get involved by supporting our school, the QSA, and the amazing and colorful drag show. Advice columnist Cassandra Duffy once said, "The beauty of standing up for your rights is others see you standing and stand up as well."

Newcomer Challenges at Mission High School

MARTINA S. * *age 18*
Mission High School

"When I came to Mission High School I was uncomfortable and I felt insecure. I knew a little bit of English, but in this country everything is different," said Gloria, a student at Mission High School. This is an experience that every student faces when they come to a new country for better opportunities. "Immigrants come for various reasons, such as to live in freedom, to escape poverty or oppression, or to make better lives for themselves," according to the website the *Gramblinite*. How can Mission High School help those students who are struggling to learn a new language?

Ms. Rodriguez, a teacher from Mission High School, said that we can help newcomer students by creating some classes that support them, and by working in the community with parents, teachers, and other people to help them. "We need to provide many experiences and opportunities for them to reach their potential in their classrooms," she said, "like after-school programs, and outside programs such as College Connect and the summer college tour." I agree with what Ms. Rodriguez said since from my own experience I have been part of those programs and they are helping me to develop successful reading and writing skills. Also, they give me advice and help prepare me for my college path.

In my own experience, I know how it feels being in a new country without knowing English and starting a new life with our family. It is an obstacle that every immigrant student has to face to continue to fight for their dreams and have a better education. We came to this country because it provides us better opportunities to make all our dreams come true.

I know from my experience that when I started in some after-school programs I did not know how to speak English, but now I feel comfortable talking with others in the language that I was struggling with at first. I am part of an after-school program, OLE, which stands for *Organización Latina Estudiantil*. By having us do some presentations, this program increased my confidence in speaking English.

Ms. Rodriguez said that this is true for other students. "OLE really helps Spanish-speaking students to know more about Mission High School and every different culture. Education is one of the factors to create more equality."

This support is very important because people should know more about some of the problems that students at Mission High School are facing. Many students pass through a challenge where they have to learn a new language and it is really hard for them because they are learning a second language. This should matter to teachers because they can support those students in fulfilling their dreams. They can encourage newcomer students to develop vital skills to impact a society that is losing the most important economic and cultural resource: bilingualism.

This section answers all kinds of important questions: If hope were a plant, which plant would it be? What's the meaning of family? What would a forgotten candle say to us? What's the best recipe for a family vacation (hint: it includes 1,000 gallons of nachos)? What kind of training camp do pencils go through? Turn the page and find out for yourself! ✽

Hope Is a Blossom Tree

Musings, Monologues, and Miscellany

Hope's Color

MAYA S. * *age 8*
St. Peter's Elementary School

Hope is something that lets you know that you should never give up. It could be explained in many ways like in plants, animals, and especially colors. Colors remind you of many things. They tell you feelings and memories, but also hope. Hope is like the color purple, dark but bright, smooth but rough. If hope were a plant it'd be a blossom tree, if it were an animal it would be a wolf, and if it were a saying it would be "just do it." So you see, hope could be explained in many ways, but it's truly just what you think and how you feel about it.

The Meaning of Family (a News Article)

AARON T. ✳ *age 16*
Woodside International High School

LOCAL SUBURBAN FAMILIES TORN APART AND BROUGHT BACK TOGETHER BY DEMON APOCALYPSE TEN YEARS AGO

In Washington D.C., eight-year-old Jax Mizumi was heading to a friend's house on June 7, 2008, at 5:00 p.m. when, all of a sudden, big, black circles appeared at every spot in the sky. That moment was when the world turned upside down, as they turned out to be portals, transporting demons through from the Underworld. This resulted in a massacre of over half of the human race. Forced into a corner, Jax had to murder his now-demon parents with his own hands. As he struggled to recover from this tragic event, his sister Laura was astonished by his pinpoint accuracy. As a result, she recruited Jax as a young member of the Apocalyptic Military Force, or AMF, to help get rid of the demons and restore humanity.

"It'll take some long, hard work, but I believe that I can turn this boy into a hero. A hero of this world," said Laura Mizumi, elder sister of Jax and Head Private of AMF.

"WOOHOO! I can't believe that actually worked! Now I can finally get some space!" Demon Number Twenty-Nine said.

Today, ten years later, eighteen-year-old Jax Mizumi is now a B-rank private and leader of a four-man team with his older sister, the Lieutenant General, as their supervisor. They also have a new addition to their family, as they rescued a boy five years earlier, who is now their new brother. But now, even as everything is going well for Jax, there is still one huge problem for him, one that'll definitely decide life or death. It's only one word, and that word . . . is *teamwork* . . .

"He's an excellent, brilliant soldier to have working for us. However, I am worried. For teamwork has proven to be quite a challenge for him," Laura Mizumi said.

"It's not my fault! I mean, it's not like I don't like them. It's just . . . I can't do well in a team. I'd rather just work solo . . ." said Jax.

His problem with teamwork will definitely become a huge issue as the population's declining and enemies are getting stronger. Getting extra help may be Jax's only path to survival, but how can they do that if they can't even get along?

As they continued with their missions and struggles, the team found out about Jax's reasons for not being able to cooperate with a team. He didn't want to lose those close to him again, as he had ten years ago. What surprised Jax was how his teammates scolded him for his reasons. It was that day when he realized that he's not the only one. They had all experienced the same tragedies that day, and are still trying to recover from those horrific times.

"I feel like such an idiot . . . I mean, I was so caught up in my own mess that I didn't even realize that we all went through the same stuff that day. I really hope that they can forgive me . . ." Jax said.

As they talked the whole situation out, they bonded more, and not only became good teammates, but a family as well.

Family is more than the people you live with. It's also those who are close to you. Those who you don't ever want to lose.

Monologue: Forgotten Candle

HONGTIAN C. ✳ *age 18*
San Francisco International High School

I am just a piece of wax covered with dust and spider webs under the bed. I don't know why I exist. I am useless. My friends, Spider and Bed, told me I should be proud of myself and cherish my life, but I am so confused. People don't even remember where I am.

I keep being depressed and upset until one night, all the lights in the house are instantly off. I can't see and I have no idea what's going on. People hurry to take me out from under the bed. Then, something unexpected happens. They wipe the dust off from me. It's comforting that someone touches me softly and cleans me up, but I wonder why they do this.

Everywhere is soaked with darkness. I hear a child yelling and crying. Then, I feel warmth on my head and it flows through my body. I am ignited by a lighter. I am lit. I am the light. I illuminate the whole house and the child stops crying. I can't believe the light from me is so bright. I am happy to see smiles on their cheeks when they continue having dinner. I know the reason why I exist. I help somebody. I understand what my friends told me. My body is gradually turning to smoke and disappears in the air. My life will end soon, but I feel proud and satisfied because I gave what they needed most at this moment. I give them my light and my life.

Wall of Hell, Door of Freedom

BRANDON F. * *age 16*
Mission High School

Dear President,

I remember you saying, "I will build a great wall—and nobody builds walls better than me, believe me—and I'll build them very inexpensively. I will build a great, great wall on our southern border, and I will make Mexico pay for that wall. Mark my words."

But every wall has a door, a door to get in; why not just build a great, great door? This door includes a better system, a better future when you open it. Not twenty shots on your back, or a broken knee from walking over twenty miles.

My mother, a Central American, Guatemalan woman, drank water from a cow's tank. She tells me, *"Caminamos por dos días, sin agua y sin comida. Nos encontramos en una granja de vacas y tomamos del agua salada de las vacas. Mientras una persona la estaba colando con la camisa mugrienta, el otro tenía las manos abajo y tomaba unas gotas, antes que el dueño se de cuenta y nos saque."* (We walked for two days, without water and without food. We found a cow farm and drank the salty water of the cows. Meanwhile, one person was filtering the water with their dirty shirt, another one had their hands underneath to get some drops of water, before the owner came and kicked us out.) My mom is capable of going to hell and back. I'd better say that every immigrant is strong enough to go to hell and back.

After crossing the fancy border line, even after they have settled in the cities they live in, any sound of a barking dog or a helicopter in the sky triggers their PTSD. They're afraid of getting shot, getting bit, getting kicked out. The immigrant life is not how our teachers have taught us. It's not like a video game, where you still have extra lives when you die and can continue or start all over.

The immigrant, "low-race" life is not easy. You don't get privileges, you don't get appreciated. Instead you're mistreated, you're stereotyped, you're marginalized. Don't build a wall, build a door that is open to the community. A door to a future, a door of freedom.

Mark my words, Mr. President.

Home Life

AMYAH H. * *17*
Downtown High School

*A young African American girl tells the story of a close friend
she empathizes with. They attend the same school. She real-
izes that not everyone has the same home and family
environment.*

When I was in the fifth grade, I went to school with a girl
named Ashley. She was a grade younger, but we were still
good friends. She was a nice person and everyone liked her.
We hung out at lunch and at the after-school program on
most days. I noticed that Ashley and her older sister would
miss school a couple days out of the week. One day, I asked
her why she would miss so much and she said that she was
either sick, or her parents couldn't take her. I thought it was
weird because my mom never let me stay home from school.
She was really smart and she did well in school, but she didn't
come for the full week.

One day after school, we were playing outside in our
program and Ashley's best friend Jaime came up to her. She
told her that her mom said she couldn't go over to her house
again, and she shouldn't be talking to her anymore. Ashley
asked, "Why?" Then, Jaime told her that her mom said that
it wasn't safe and she wouldn't be comfortable letting her

stay there. At that time, I had never gone to her house, so I didn't know what she was talking about. I was confused.

A couple weeks passed after Jaime told her that. On a Saturday, Ashley called me and asked if I wanted to come over and see her dog's new puppies. I asked my dad to take me and he agreed. He drove me over to her house. It was on the other side of the city, so I had never been there. The area had garbage everywhere and boarded up houses. When we got there, my dad walked me up halfway, then asked what time he had to get me and left. I rang the doorbell and waited. While I was waiting, I saw some red and brown stuff on the ground. I was wondering what it was because I wasn't used to just seeing blood on the ground. Her mom opened the door and apologized for it and explained how it got there. She said the landlord fought someone who stayed below them.

After I met her mom, I could tell that she was doing drugs. I stepped over it, kind of scared, and walked in. I noticed that the house was dark and cold. She apologized again and told me why the power was out. It was out because they didn't have enough money to pay for it. I didn't judge her because it wasn't my place and I was a good friend, so I stayed. We started to walk to her room and there was cardboard, spider webs, and blankets everywhere. The house had a weird scent. We went in and looked at the puppies for a while then she showed me around the house. We looked through every room. We went into the kitchen and everything was thrown in there and there was some animal in there, so her mom told us to go to the park. After we got back from the park my dad was there to pick me up. I was somewhat relieved to see him.

When I got home, I told my dad and called my mom to tell her I got home. She was visiting my auntie for a couple of days, so I had to call. My mom was mad for a second. Then, she started to feel bad for Ashley and her older sister who were living there. When she got home a couple days later, we talked about it. Then, we realized why Ashley was always sick and couldn't make it to school. She was sick because her house had no heat and she couldn't get better staying there. Another reason she couldn't make it to school was because her mom wasn't there all the time and her dad worked day and night to support her family and the dogs. A couple weeks after I went to her house, she stopped going to school. I got worried and asked some teachers at my school, but they said they couldn't tell me where she was and why she was absent.

I forgot about it that summer. The next school year, I started middle school, and in the middle of that year, I saw her older sister. So, I stopped her and asked how she was doing and where they went. She told me they had to go to a foster home, so they switched their schools. They went to foster care because of the way they were living and because their mom was on drugs. I only saw her about three times that year and after that she stopped going. I don't know where they went, but I still see their mom walking around the Mission.

A Family Vacation

ROBERTO R. * *age 9*
Buena Vista Horace Mann

INGREDIENTS

1,000 gallons of nachos

100 cups of Oreos

100 gallons of swimming

10 teaspoons of song

1,000,000 gallons of laughing

7 cups of sleeping

50 tablespoons of jumping on the bed

1,000 cups of free time

1,000,000,000 gallons of dabbing

DIRECTIONS

To make a family vacation, pour the ingredients into a hotel. Taste the Oreos. The Oreos will taste so good! Then, chop the nachos and add them to the swimming, laughing, and jumping on the bed. Add water and mix them together in the pot. It makes the vacation healthy for you. Then add a pinch of the song and bake them together with the free time and dabbing. It will make you laugh so hard. And then add most of the sleeping. Fry and flip over. It will be so good.

My Appreciation

LAYLAY D. * *age 17*
Downtown High School

A young black girl is talking to her aunt in the living room of their home as she prepares to take off, telling her things she never told her before, and letting her know that she is appreciated.

I would like to thank you, Auntie, for all that you have done. I hope to be as strong as you when I am older. You are a great a definition of awesome, you're even better than music. There were times I put you through stuff you never should have had to deal with, being that I was not your responsibility. All the fights and arguments with you were not necessary. The phone calls home and skipping school—I apologize for it all.

Along the way, it wasn't all bad. Auntie, you've taught me a lot of life lessons, like "Watch your temper," and "Change your attitude." You also let me know that college should be an option and you taught me ways to think about it. You told me that I should attend college for as many years that I need for the career that I want—not just four years.

I do appreciate you, if you know it or not. I appreciate you teaching me how to cook, telling me, "Always keep the fire low, a good meal takes time." I appreciate you being there every time, when no one else was. I appreciate you being just like a mom to me. I appreciate you teaching me right from wrong. After all the bad and the struggles I brought to you, you are still with me. You still love me and you are there because you know I need someone to be there to support me in my every step. I appreciate that most.

Yesterday Was Summer, Today Is Fall, and Tomorrow Is Winter

YAHIR A. * *age 10*
Thomas Edison Charter Academy

Okay, okay . . . Days like these, I feel like every day is a new season. Yesterday was summer, today is fall, and tomorrow is winter. By that, I mean that it was so hot last week, but this week was breezy.

When I watch the news for the weather, it says it's going to be cold tomorrow. When I go to school, it's the dawn of summer where it feels like a week and we are all waiting for fall. We are happy. The eclipse, school days, Halloween, and all of those days felt like they were squashed in one day because the days have been fast, especially the weekends.

I bet some of the readers reading this agree. It's not just that. In the new year when 2017 came, I expected it would take about a whole decade to finish a year, but it felt like a month.

It's not just that. I'm ten years old, which means that I'm a decade old, but becoming ten years old might feel like a year.

I bet if I was able to survive for an entire century, it would feel like a decade, going back to a day, a normal day.

In conclusion of this, I think that time goes so fast, but thankfully it ends when daylight savings ends on November 5, Sunday, at 2:00 a.m. To end this, one bonus conclusion: *Time goes about mach 10,000* (the same speed as sound).

Out of the Haze

CHLOE K. * *age 17*
Lowell High School

EXT. LOCKER ROOMS, DAY

Two doors, big, red, strong enough to get through any break-in. One is marked "Girls," the other "Boys." It's unmistakable. They're the locker rooms.

It's a dangerous place, filled with lock-snatchers and prepubescents that have yet to discover the magic of deodorant. The doors bursts open.

The Girls' door reveals a squealing, squalling, gaggle of ponytailed teenagers ready for a class filled with gossip, maybe some sports thrown in there.

Buried among them is Savannah, his long hair pushed over his eyes.

Then the boys burst out, running towards the field. Savannah stops and watches them.

They're big, burly, muscular, football-magazine spread ready cardboard cut-outs of the sports star golden boy. Watch out ladies, here come the heartbreakers.

ZOOM OUT. EXT. FOOTBALL FIELD, DAY

The girls are clustered in their ever sacred conversation circles, pretending they aren't watching the boys.

Savannah stands off to the side, no spot in a circle for him. He watches the boys, too, but doesn't bother hiding where he's looking.

GIRL 1: Oh my god, was he looking at me?

GIRL 2: In your dreams.

GIRL 1: No seriously, I think he was!

GIRL 3: Okay, so I got my prom dress right—

GIRL 1: Shhh, I think one of them is watching me.

GIRL 3: But it's like, way too tight in the bust, you know?

GIRL 2: Oh, shut up!

GIRL 3: What, it's a real problem!

GIRL 1: Oh my god, was he looking at me? Sidney, check it out, I totally think he was looking at me.

GIRL 2: No, he was definitely looking at me that time.

Savannah, overhearing their conversation, lets out a snort.

GIRL 2: *(to Savannah)* What are you looking at?

SAVANNAH: Nothing, sorry.

GIRL 2 wrinkles her nose at Savannah, like he's something nasty stuck to the bottom of her shoe. Intimidation factor on all-time high. Slowly, she turns back to her friends.

Relieved, Savannah turns his gaze back to the boys.

He stares dead on. The same way a baby stares, unapologetic and curious. He doesn't fluff his hair or bat his eyes.

DAY DREAM: *Savannah sees himself amongst them, short hair now, walking tall and proud, winning the stares of boys and girls alike. He's the golden boy. Everyone wants a piece of him. A scream pulls Savannah back to reality.*

For the first time, the camera focuses on the other end of the spectrum on high school boys who are currently streaming out of the locker room.

Stuck among the golden boys are the lowly, the nerdy, the get-pimples-on-your-nose-for-pushing-up-your-glasses-type. One day they'll be millionaires—or some of them at least—but today is not that day.

They're pushed, they're shoved, they're trampled amongst the sneakers of boys much stronger than them.

One of them has been pushed to the ground, and is fighting back tears.

Savannah wipes his palms, now slick with sweat, on the red polyester of his gym shorts. Should he intervene?

He takes a step forward, his sneaker making an indent on the turf.

DAY DREAM: *The dream is back, Savannah amongst the golden boys. But he is no longer one of them. Now, he is the nerd pushed to the ground. He's trampled, stomped, mangled, drowning in a mass of limbs and polyester gym shorts. He hears the jeering of thousands of voices, all directed at him. And there's nothing he can do.*

GIRL 1: Hey watch out!

Savannah jumps, pulled back into reality. Just in time to get hit in the face with an oncoming ball.

CUT TO INT. LESLIE'S CAR, DAY

Savannah sits next to his mom, LESLIE, holding an ice pack to his head. His mom sits in the driver's seat.

The car is parked. An awkward silence ensues, Leslie waiting for her kid to speak.

LESLIE: So are you going to tell me why I had to pick you up from the nurse's office?

A beat. Savannah shrugs.

LESLIE: Or am I just going to have to guess?

SAVANNAH: *(mumbles)* Ball hit me.

LESLIE: Okay, why?

Savannah shrugs again.

SAVANNAH: It was moving, I wasn't. Then I got hit.

Exasperated, Leslie sighs. She turns the car key, starting the engine and pulls out from her parking spot outside of the school.

The two ride in silence.

SAVANNAH: Hey Mom?

LESLIE: Mmhm?

SAVANNAH: Can we move?

Leslie rolls her eyes.

A Grand Killer

MAX T. ✳ *age 9*
George Moscone Elementary School

Something orange, sometimes it is big, other times small, sometimes killer, and sometimes friendly. You can hear its screams. And if you smell it, you can even come to death. It's the same if you taste. You come to death, and don't even think of touching it!

FIRE!

Take the Shot! It's Open!

KAMRON P. * *age 17*
Downtown High School

A basketball speaks to his owner about how their relationship
is important to keep him in school. The basketball does not
want him to drop out. They are in the gym where the ball is
trying to convince the young man to go back to class.

What do you want? I see you looking at me like you're ready
to give up! I know you are addicted to me or something, but
what are you waiting for? Why have you been cutting yourself short? Missing class and not going to practice ain't what's
gonna get you to varsity. I've seen what you got, and you know
coach really wants you on the team. I know you have the
commitment for this sport. I know being in the NBA has been
one of your dreams since you were a kid. But your lack of
actions are holding you back from getting into the playoffs.
You need to be in class right now, and not here playing hoops!
You need to understand that being successful in school is
going to lead to your success in basketball and the team.

Do you doubt yourself? Or do you not see yourself being
a hooper? Forget that! We both know you have a lot of room
for improvement, but you love me and the sport! You can't
ever see yourself without me. It's all work. Every job or move

you make, it's another dribble move you have to master. Just like in school, every move you make determines your outcome. Easy like a layup! All you gotta do is show up! What's stoppin' you from blocking the opponent? Don't be afraid to defend the bigger player, because you're bigger and better than him. It shouldn't be the reason why you get booted from the team.

Take the shot! It's open! I've been with you this whole time and I've watched you be successful. We've won games together, we've conditioned together, been through the hard times together. I ain't planning to give up on you now. Don't wait 'til the end of the shot clock! It's time to go hard in the paint and take the game-winning shot. Remember you don't have to do this on your own. You have teammates who can help get you through this game of life. Trust me. Take the shot! It's open!

The Last Pencil in the Box

EDWARD G. * *age 18*
Mission High School

"All pencils up. Salute," said the Colonel. "Six a.m. and we have to train for writing and success. We have run over bumpy roads, been kicked, and have gone through the human grinder—the mouth of a child—which is a very common place to end up. That is why we have to be hard like a rock."

"Today we will enter the simulator, the pencil sharpener, a place where we leave our childhood and enter adulthood. It's only a simulator for now, soldiers, nothing to worry about. Soldier Rudy, tell me a goal."

"We are meant to sting like a bee, fly like a butterfly, and swim like a shark."

"Did you just say swim, soldier?"

"Yes, sir."

"Medical group, check his eraser," the Colonel said, "He might have a stiff brain."

"Now, like I was saying, soldiers, each of you is a machine. Soldier Bob, what are we here for?"

"We are here to write and erase, sir."

"Excellent, Bob."

Several years later, Soldier Rudy said to himself, "Finally, I got chosen. I'm the last pencil in the box. I need to remember my goal—sting like a bee, fly like a . . . Wait, wait a minute, that's not right. My goal is to write, erase, and be part of the student's success."

"Soon I will be in the dark place, in the backpack heading to school. This is our destiny. We either end up in the classroom battlefield, where most soldiers give their lives, or we get lost in the halls of schools, where we get kicked into a corner with old friends and comrades."

The Black Sky and the Star

ASMA A. * *age 10*
Cross Cultural Family Center of San Francisco

The star says to the black sky in a teasing voice, "You are not as bright as me."

The black sky says, "You are making me feel sad and left behind."

The star says, "Then why can't you be as bright as me?"

The black sky laughs and answers, "Without me, you wouldn't be as bright as you are now."

The star thinks for a moment and replies, "That is true. Black Sky, without you, I wouldn't be bright."

The star felt thankful because of the black sky.

Warrior Bird

ALIZON L. * *age 11*
Everett Middle School

Oh quetzal, *you* seem so strong as a warrior bird with your shade of blue, flying like a powerful bird. In the sky, you seem so sneaky to take your place in Guatemala and shine as the state bird.

You made it! You're probably thinking, "Phew! Now I know every single thing that happens at 826 Valencia. There's nothing more to know." And that's where you're wrong. There are more people and projects involved in a single week at 826 than we could fit in this entire book. Just imagine that for every name, publication, and program listed in the coming pages, there are a few hundred names of volunteers, too. This may sound fantastic, but you just finished reading *the 826 Quarterly.* Your imagination should be pretty limbered up now. ✻

826 Valencia

Who We Are and What We Do

THE 826 QUARTERLY * VOL. 26

Who We Are

STAFF

Bita Nazarian *Executive Director*

Brad Amorosino *Design Director*

Alyssa Aninag *Volunteer Coordinator*

Dana Belott *Programs Coordinator*

Nicole C. Brown *Individual Philanthropy Officer*

Elaina Bruna *Development Coordinator*

Ricardo Cruz-Chong *Programs Associate*

Precediha Dangerfield *Programs Coordinator*

Shelby Dale DeWeese *Programs Coordinator*

Allyson Halpern *Development Director*

Virdell Hickman *Operations Manager*

Caroline Kangas *Stores Manager*

Kona Lai *Programs Coordinator*

Kiley McLaughlin *Programs Coordinator*

Molly Parent *Communications and Programs Manager*

Christina V. Perry *Director of Education*

Kathleen Rodriguez *Tutoring Programs Manager*

Meghan Ryan *Publications Manager*

Ashley Smith *Programs Manager*

Megan Waring *Intern Coordinator*

Jillian Wasick *Programs Manager*

Byron Weiss *Assistant Stores Manager*

Leah Tarlan *Director, Institutional Gifts*

Anton Timms *Volunteer Engagement Director*

Ryan Young *In-Schools Programs Manager*

AMERICORPS SUPPORT STAFF

Through Summer 2018

Melissa Anguiano *Buena Vista Horace Mann Programs Associate*
Angelina Brand *Field Trips and After-School Tutoring Associate*
Katie Cugno *In-Schools Programs Associate*
Lila Cutter *Volunteer Engagement Associate*
Izel Jimenez *After-School Programs Associate*
Paloma Mariz *Communications Associate*
Olivia Ortiz *Development and Evaluations Associate*
Steph Yun *Tenderloin Programs Associate*

STORE STAFF

Antoinette Barton

Alexandra Cotrim

Isabel Craik

Tim R.

OUR BELOVED INTERNS

Spring 2017

Monica Bonilla

Helena Chow

Megan Cliff

Maeve Donovan

Hagar Elgafy

Michael Franklin

Laurel Fujii

Christine Innes

Judy Hart

Priscilla Leung

Mia Lai Leynes

Lindsay Mamet

Edda Marcos

Shanika Mari
   Badoya-Mulkerin

Josette Marsh

Ty Mecozzi

Jake Murphy

Sean Nishi

Tanner Reyes

Molly Schellenger

Michael Scott Petitte

Aimee Sun Kwon

Summer 2017

Elizabeth Arnett

Rose Bialer

Luke Davis

Lesley Gonzalez

Zoe Harris

Morgan Hartig

Christine Innes

Casey Jong

Sayon Latoyha

Mia Lai Leynes

Kaitlin Lang

Heidi Maqueos

OUR VOLUNTEERS

There's absolutely no way we could create hundreds of publications and serve thousands of students annually without a legion of volunteers. These incredible people work in all realms, from tutoring to fundraising and beyond. They range in age, background, and expertise but all have a shared passion for our work with young people. Volunteers past and present, you know who you are. Thank you, thank you, thank you.

826 NATIONAL

826 Valencia's success has spread across the country. Under the umbrella of 826 National, writing and tutoring centers have opened in six more cities. If you would like to learn more about other 826 programs, please visit the following websites.

826 National	**826DC**	**826NYC**
826national.org	826dc.org	826nyc.org
826 Boston	**826LA**	**826 Valencia**
826boston.org	826la.org	826valencia.org
826CHI	**826michigan**	
826chi.org	826michigan.org	

What We Do

826 Valencia is a nonprofit organization dedicated to supporting under-resourced students ages six to eighteen with their creative and expository writing skills and to helping teachers inspire their students to write. Our services are structured around the understanding that great leaps in learning can happen with one-on-one attention and that strong writing skills are fundamental to future success.

826 Valencia comprises two writing centers—our flagship location in the Mission District and a new center in the Tenderloin neighborhood—and three satellite classrooms at nearby schools. Both of our centers are fronted by kid-friendly, weird, and whimsical stores, which serve as portals to learning and gateways for the community. All of our programs are offered free of charge. Since we first opened our doors in 2002, thousands of volunteers have dedicated their time to working with tens of thousands of students.

PROGRAMS

Field Trips

Classes from public schools around San Francisco visit our writing centers for a morning of high-energy learning about the craft of storytelling. Four days a week, our Field Trips produce bound, illustrated books and professional-quality podcasts, infusing creativity, collaboration, and the arts into students' regular school day.

In-Schools Programs

We bring teams of volunteers into high-need schools around the city to support teachers and provide one-on-one assistance to students as they tackle various writing projects, including newspapers, research papers, oral histories, and more. We have a special presence at Buena Vista Horace Mann K–8, Everett Middle School, and Mission High School, where we staff dedicated Writers' Rooms throughout the school year.

After-School Tutoring

During the school year, 826 Valencia's centers are packed five days a week with neighborhood students who come in after school and in the evenings for tutoring in all subject areas, with a special emphasis on creative writing and publishing. During the summer these students participate in our five-week Exploring Words Summer Camp, where we explore science and writing through projects, outings, and activities in a super fun educational environment.

Workshops

826 Valencia offers workshops designed to foster creativity and strengthen writing skills in a wide variety of areas, from playwriting to personal essays to starting a 'zine. All workshops, from the playful to the practical, are project-based and are taught by experienced, accomplished professionals. Over the summer, our Young Authors' Workshop provides a two-week intensive writing experience for high-school-age students.

College and Career Readiness

We offer a roster of programs designed to help students get into college and be successful there. Every year we provide six $15,000 scholarships to college-bound seniors, provide one-on-one support to two hundred students via the Great

San Francisco Personal Statement Weekend, and partner with ScholarMatch to offer college access workshops to the middle- and high-school students in our tutoring programs. We also offer internships, peer tutoring stipends, and career workshops to our youth leaders.

Publishing

Students in all of 826 Valencia's programs have the ability to explore, experience, and celebrate themselves as writers in part because of our professional-quality publishing. In addition to the book you're holding, 826 Valencia publishes newspapers, magazines, chapbooks, podcasts, and blogs—all written by students.

Teacher of the Month

From the beginning, 826 Valencia's goal has been to support teachers. We aim to both provide the classroom support that helps our hardworking teachers meet the needs of all our students and to celebrate their important work. Every month, we receive letters from students, parents, and educators nominating outstanding teachers for our Teacher of the Month award, which comes with a $1,500 honorarium. Know an SFUSD teacher you want to nominate? Guidelines can be found at 826valencia.org.

Other Books from 826 Valencia

826 Valencia produces a variety of publications, each of which contains work written by students in our programs. Some are professionally printed and nationally distributed; others are glued together here and sold in our stores. These projects represent some of the most exciting work at 826 Valencia, as they enable Bay Area students to experience a world of publishing not otherwise available to them. The following is a selection of publications available for purchase at our stores, online at 826valencia.org/store, or through your local bookstore:

 *We Are Here, Walking Toward the Unknown* (2017) is a collection of narrative essays about adapting from students at Phillip & Sala Burton Academic High School. Have you ever been misunderstood or judged? What fears are you working to overcome? Can science and technology go too far? If you had the opportunity to go back, how would you fix a past mistake? While these questions were inspired by the themes in Mary Shelley's Frankenstein, a book written in the nineteenth century, they are still as thought-provoking and relevant as ever. In this collection, the seniors of Burton High in San Francisco set out to answer them in the form of personal narratives, fictional short stories,

and letters. From intimate reflections about their own lived experiences, to the development of creative and futuristic worlds, these young authors meditate on our past, present, and future—and the results prove illuminating for all.

Walk the Earth in Our Shoes and Plant Some Seeds Behind You (2016) collects personal essays from students at John O'Connell High School. What would we learn if we could interview a whale? Is diversity as advantageous in a social community as it is in a coral reef? How does our environment affect us, and how do we affect our environment? These questions are both age-old and urgent, and in this collection, ninth- and tenth-grade authors set out to answer them. From how their neighborhoods are changing to what it's like to live in a drought, these young authors share their views and experiences as they investigate the way ecosystems work—and their answers hold insights everyone should read.

If the World Only Knew (2015) is a collection of essays written by sixty-six freshmen at Mission High School. In this book students reflect on their beliefs and where they come from—the people who imparted them, the times when they were most necessary, and the ways in which the world has tested them. The collection is a testament to the power of personal conviction, and a powerful case for why young peoples' voices should be heard —and believed.

Uncharted Places (2014) is a collection of essays by fifty-two juniors and seniors at Thurgood Marshall High School that examines the idea of "place" and what it means to these young authors. It contains stories about locales real and imagined, internal and external, places of transition and those of comfort. These young writers bravely share their views of the world, giving us a glimpse into the places that are most important to them —those not necessarily found on a map, but in the heart.

 *Beyond Stolen Flames, Forbidden Fruit, and Telephone Booths* (2011) is a collection of essays and short stories, written by fifty-three juniors and seniors at June Jordan School for Equity, in which young writers explore the role of myth in our world today. Students wrote pieces of fiction and nonfiction, retelling old myths, creating new ones, celebrating everyday heroes, and recognizing the tales that their families have told over and over. With a foreword by Khaled Hosseini, the result is a collection with a powerful message about the stories that have shaped students' perspectives and the world they know.

 *Show of Hands* (2009) is a collection of stories and essays written by fifty-four juniors and seniors at Mission High School. It amplifies the students' voices as they reflect on one of humanity's most revered guides for moral behavior: the Golden Rule, which tells us that we should act toward others as we would want them to act toward us. Whether speaking about global issues, street violence, or the way to behave among friends and family, the voices of these young essayists are brilliant, thoughtful, and, most of all, urgent.

Thanks and Have Fun Running the Country (2009) is a collection of letters penned by our After-School Tutoring students to newly-elected President Obama. In this collection, which arrived at inauguration time, there's loads of advice for the president, often hilarious, sometimes heartfelt, and occasionally downright practical. The letters have been featured in *The New York Times*, the *San Francisco Chronicle*, and on *This American Life*.

I Live Real Close to Where You Used to Live (2010) is a collection of letters to Michelle, Sasha, Malia, and Bo Obama written by students across the 826 network. These letters are packed with questions, advice, and the occasional request to be invited over to the White House for dinner.

Exactly (2007) is a hardbound book of colorful stories for children ages nine to eleven. This collection of fifty-six narratives by students at Raoul Wallenberg Traditional High School is illustrated by forty-three professional artists. It passes on lessons that teenagers want the next generation to know.

EDUCATOR RESOURCES

Don't Forget to Write (2005) contains fifty-four of the best lesson plans used in workshops taught at 826 Valencia, 826NYC, and 826LA, giving away all of our secrets for making writing fun. Each lesson plan was written by its original workshop teacher, including Jonathan Ames, Aimee Bender, Dave Eggers, Erika Lopez, Julie Orringer, Jon Scieszka, Sarah Vowell, and many others. If you are a parent or a teacher, this book is meant to make your life easier, as it contains enthralling and effective ideas to get your students writing. It can also be used as a resource for the aspiring writer. In 2011, 826 National published a two-volume second edition of *Don't Forget to Write*, also available in our stores.

STEM to Story (2015) contains dynamic lesson plans that use hands-on discovery and creative writing to teach students about science, technology, math, and engineering. These quirky, exploratory lessons are sure to awaken the imagination and ignite passions for both STEM and creative writing. *STEM to Story* is a boon to teachers, parents, and students alike, as each lesson plan is aligned with Common Core and Next Gen Science Standards.

Our Supporters

We couldn't do this work without the generosity of our donors, including our 2016-2017 leadership supporters, who provide needed essential funding to all of our diverse writing programs where student writing and student voice is cultivated and celebrated. This biannual anthology is a reflection of students across our programs and the important stories they have to tell.

CAPTAIN

Anonymous (3)

826 National

Acton Family Giving

Advisors of the Walnut Fund

Marc and Lynne Benioff

Bothin Foundation

The Brin Wojcicki
Foundation

The Callison Foundation

Cameron Schrier Family Fund

City Arts & Lectures

Coltrane and Christopher
Lord Fund

Tom Conrad

In memory of Alberto Curotto

Different Fur Studios

Dolby Laboratories

ExCEL After School Programs

Lee and Russ Flynn

Daniel Handler and Lisa Brown

The HBO *Crashing* Tour

Frances Hellman and
Warren Breslau

Hellman Foundation

Horace W. Goldsmith
Foundation

The Kimball Foundation

Kochi Foundation

Lampert/Byrd Family Fund

Lisa & Douglas Goldman Fund

Maverick Capital Foundation

Panta Rhea Foundation

Scott Patterson

Pincus Family Fund of the
Silicon Valley Community
Foundation

Arthur and Toni Rembe Rock

San Francisco Department
of Children, Youth, and
Their Families

San Francisco Office of
Economic and Workforce
Development

Sara and Evan Williams
Foundation

Tom Savignano

Severns Family Foundation

Michael and Shauna Stark

Laurie and Jeff Ubben

W.L.S. Spencer Foundation

Karen and Jim Wagstaffe

Walter and Elise Haas Fund

FIRST MATE

Anonymous

Colleen Quinn Amster and
John Amster

Joya Banerjee and Harris Cohen

BBDO San Francisco

Michael and Kirsten Beckwith

Randie Bencanann and
Bobby Baron

Art Berliner and Marian Lever

The Bernard Osher Foundation

Dominique Bischoff-Brown
as a gift for Different Fur
Studios and Patrick Brown

Crescent Porter Hale
Foundation

Darren Delaye and
Jaime Huling Delaye

Ian and Keri Ferry

Fineshriber Foundation

Fleishhacker Foundation

glassybaby white light fund

Graybird Foundation

Hall Capital Partners Fund

Parker Harris and Holly Johnson

Christina Hurvis and Steve Malloy

Vy and Matthew Hyman

Kimberly and Zachary Hyman

Diana Kapp and David Singer

Jim and Tricia Lesser

Marc and Jamie Lunder

Microsoft

Michael Moritz and
Harriet Heyman

Dave and Gina Pell

Janet and Clint Reilly

Remick Family Foundation

Robin Renfrew and family
in honor of Taylor Renfrew
Ingham

The Rose and David
Dortort Foundation

Sakana Foundation

San Francisco Unified
School District

Twitter

The Walther Foundation

Warriors Community
Foundation

Eli and Leigha Weinberg

Kevin and Rachel Yeaman

SHIP'S MASTER

Anonymous

Alex and Diana Adamson

Alexander M. & June L.
Maisin Foundation of the
Jewish Community Federation
and Endowment Fund

Alice Beckett

Arlene Buechert

Charles Slaughter and
Molly West Fund

Clark R. Smith Family
Foundation

Curran Theatre

The David C. and Lura M. Lovell
Foundation

Nasseam Elkarra

Erwin Hosono and Beth Axelrod

Jessica Goldman Foung

Jeri and Jeffrey Johnson

Kevin King and Meridee Moore

Alex Lerner

Orange River Fund

Kamie Pham

Mark Risher and Deborah Yeh

Brian and Kristina Schwartz

Rachel Segars

SF Sketchfest

Lee and Perry Smith Fund

Stanford Center on Philanthropy
and Civil Society

Stanley S. Langendorf
Foundation

The Stocker Foundation

Andrew Strickman and
Michal Ettinger

Third Eye Blind

Tim Tiefenthaler

Treasure Island Music Festival

David and Susan Tunnell

Mike Wilkins and Sheila Duignan

Zynga.org Foundation

BOATSWAIN

Another Planet Entertainment

Bill Graham Supporting
Foundation of the Jewish
Community Federation and
Endowment Fund

Jennifer Bunshoft Pergher

The Burnett Fund

Chambers & Chambers Wine
Merchants

The Donald and Carole
Chaiken Foundation

Vanessa and Matt Ginzton

Gundlach Bundschu and the
Huichica Music Festival

Shepard and Melissa Harris

Cristy and Rob Higgins

Joe Hill and the Friends of
Keyhouse

Derek and Pamela Howard

Gail and Ian Jardine

Melind John

Angie and Jon Keehn

Keker Family Foundation

Jacquelyn and Todd Krieger

Jordan Kurland

Frances McDormand and
Joel Coen

Pacific Gas and Electric Company

Cheryl Petersen and Frank Pine

Grant and Mary Petersen

Silicon Valley Bank

Todd Smithline

Steven Nathaniel Wolkoff
Foundation

William and Heather Terrell

Peter and Alyson Van Hardenberg

Velos Mobile LLC

Rick and Nicole Wolfgram

HELMSPERSON

Anonymous (2)

Laurel Adams

David Agger

Frank Barbieri

Marian Beard

Christopher Beckmann

David and Sarah Berger

Jeff Bluestone and
    Leah Rosenkrantz

Jennifer Braun and Ray Ryan

Tad and Emilia Buchanan

Denise and Clay Bullwinkel

Ed Cavagnaro and Barbara Goode

Lydia Chavez and Mark Rabine

The Chrysopolae Foundation

Cleaves and Mae Rhea Foundation

Kelly Close

Coach, Inc.

The Companion Group

Lionel Conacher and Joan Dea

Kathy and Patrick Coyle

David and Carla Crane
    Philanthropic Fund

David Foster Wallace
    Literary Trust

Michael Duckworth

Isabel Duffy-Pinner and
    Dickon Pinner

Rick and Holly Elfman

First Republic Bank

Carol Francis and Steve Chapman

Fred Gellert Family Foundation

Daniel Gelfand and Nicole Avril

Gelfand Partners Architects

Dan and Nikki George

Mike Glaser and
    Kristine Hernandez

Malcolm and Kopal Goonetileke

Green Bicycle Fund

Joe and Barbara Gurkoff
    Philanthropic Fund

Brent and Ryann Harris

Katie and Lee Hicks

Reece Hirsch and Kathy Taylor

Liz Hume and Jay Jacobs

Irene S. Scully Fund

J.B. Berland Foundation

June P. Jackson Charitable Fund

Mark Jacobsen and Pam Laird

Susan Karp and Paul Haahr

Puja and Samir Kaul

Jimmy Kimmel

Walter Korman

Cathy Kornblith

Jonathan Koshi and Jess Hemerly

Meg Krehbiel

Kruger Family Foundation

Michael S. Kwun and Sigrid
    Anderson-Kwun Fund

Naomi and Sharky Laguana

Gloria Lenhart

Rachel Levin and Josh Richter

Lynda Marren

Mary K. Robertson Family Fund

Donna Maynard

Steven Miller

Anna and Mason Morfit

Amir Najmi and Linda Woo

The Nancy and Sid Fund

Noise Pop Industries

Norman Raab Foundation

The Odell/Kemp Fund

Jim O'Donnell and
    Michael Ginther

Katy and David Orr

The OutCast Agency

Sejal Patel and Sanjay Banker

PECO Foundation

Tham Thao Pham and Adam Tait

James Ponsoldt

Marcia Rodgers and
    Garrett Loube

Henry and Kate Rogers

David and Erin Russell

Celia Sack and Omnivore
    Books on Food

Andy Schwab and
  Catarina Norman

Will Scullin

Stacey Silver and Jon Yolles

Juliet Starrett

The Stephen and Paula Smith
  and Kendall Wilson Family
  Foundation

Rachel and Stephen Tracy

Todd Traina

Tuft & Needle

Ron Turiello

Valencia Corridor Merchants
  Association

Ellen and Rob Valletta

Joe Vasquez

Valerie Veronin and
  Robert Porter

Vocera Corporate Fund

Brooks Walker and
  Summer Tompkins Walker

Julia Wang Sze

Eli and Lauren Weiss

Donna Williamson

Carey and Noah Wintroub

Tim Wirth and Anne Stuhldreher

Yellen/Kozak Family
  Charitable Fund

Diane Zagerman and
  Donald Golder

Kristine and Rob Zehner

Ben Zotto

SAILOR

Nicole Boyer

Andrew Dunbar and
  Zoee Astrachan

John Eidinger

Allyson Halpern and Dan Cohen

Dean Huynh

Garrett Kamps

Killing My Lobster

Joshua J. Mahoney

John Schlag and Jennifer Gennari

Mary Taylor

It's Always a Good Time to Give

WE NEED YOUR HELP

We could not do this work without the thousands of volunteers who make our programs possible. We are always seeking more volunteer tutors, and volunteers with design, illustration, and photography skills. It's easy to become a volunteer and a bunch of fun to actually do it.

Please fill out our online application to let us know how you'd like to lend your time:
826valencia.org/get-involved/volunteer

OTHER WAYS TO GIVE

Whether it's loose change or heaps of cash, a donation of any size will help 826 Valencia continue to offer a variety of free writing and publishing programs to Bay Area youth.

Please make a donation at:
826valencia.org/donate

You can also mail your contribution to:
826 Valencia Street, San Francisco, CA 94110

Your donation is tax-deductible. What a plus! Thank you!